Rocky Mountain Ghost

Kurt James

DEDICATION

*For my Uncle Larry McCall Patton.
When I was little, I always wanted to be like Uncle
Larry - to look like him and to have his sense of humor.
He will be missed by others. I will miss him! I loved
him! He was my hero....*

Kurt James

ACKNOWLEDGMENTS

Without the help from my good friend Kurt "Wally" Wollenweber I would never be able to follow my dream of being a storyteller.

Disclaimer

Kurt James

Rocky Mountain Ghost

TABLE OF CONTENTS

CHAPTER 1

I recognized the battle flag one of the troopers was carrying as belonging to the 3rd Colorado Cavalry, the same 3rd Cavalry that had been commanded by Colonel John Chivington during the "Battle of Sand Creek" that was now called the "Sand Creek Massacre." The battle was an attack and slaughter of mostly women and children in a village of Cheyenne and Arapaho Indians in the southeastern Colorado Territory on the banks of Sand Creek several years ago. Their nickname was the Bloodless 3rd, which always baffled me coming on the heels of a bloody massacre.

I raised my right hand so that Chance Bondurant, his half wolf and half something else dog Mutt, Kellie Shawn Arriaga, and Walk With Ghost would come to a halt not 100 yards away from the soldiers that were filtering through the evergreen and aspen tree line into the largest meadow in the Kawuneeche Valley in the remote Colorado Rocky Mountains many miles north of Grand Lake, Colorado.

The youngster Chance rode his mare Storm just to my left about five yards as we watched in silence as more and more troopers filtered in from the dark timber. It was several minutes before they all had emerged from the woods and I had lost count at 72, but looked less than 100 men – a lot less than a regiment, but with the makings of a full troop of 95.

We were not surprised to see them; hell we were expecting them, but they sure looked surprised to see us. After several minutes of studying us as we sat on our horses studying them, two of the soldiers peeled away and headed in our direction.

As the soldiers got closer, the one leading wore the chevron of a Master Sergeant and the one lagging beyond wore the insignia of a 1st Lieutenant. After bringing their horses to a halt about five yards in front of us, the Master Sergeant with close cropped dark hair and a full dark beard and built like a man that could handle himself with his fists, spoke in a deep and grave voice, "We are surprised to see folks so early in the spring heading down from the remote wilderness, and you have no pelts. So I assume you are not trappers?"

Since the statement was merely an observation, I said nothing in response. The Master Sergeant seemed annoyed at this and spoke again, "And?"

In an unhurried response, "And what Sergeant? You rode up to talk to us; we didn't ride down the mountain side to talk to you. If you want to ask a question, then ask it son."

The 1st Lieutenant was a hawkish and frail looking fellow, and his eyes narrowed to my response as he was not liking me at all. The Master Sergeant broke into a slight smile and with a small chuckle said, "That's fair enough. Let me start over again with some introductions. My Name is Master Sergeant Andy Cacy, and the 1st Lieutenant's name is Art Wilson. We have been given a mission to locate a band of 60 or more renegade Ute Indians that are being led by Chief Piah and to persuade them to move to a reservation out west in Utah Territory. I guess my question is have you seen this band of renegades?"

Seeing no harm in telling the truth, "Yes, we wintered with them and just left them several days ago. I thought the 3rd

Colorado Cavalry had been disbanded after the shutdown of Fort Collins and Fort Lyons.

Master Sergeant Andy Cacy looked a little confused by my statement when he replied, "They had been disbanded but reformed when this Indian rebellion began. Do you mind pointing us in the right direction toward their winter camp?"

Shaking my head "no" before I replied, "That I cannot do. Chief Piah is my brother-in-law and he would not be happy with me if I pointed the U.S. Cavalry in his direction. I am positive with as many men as you got, you will stumble across them sometime soon."

The smile disappeared from Master Sergeant Andy Cacy's face, "If we let you leave, how will we be assured that you won't double back and warn your brother-in-law that we are in the Kawuneeche Valley looking for his tribe of renegades?"

Both Chance and I started to chuckle at the same time and exchanged a glance before I spoke again, "Hell, Master Sergeant the Ute Indians, as savage as they can be, are not stupid. Look around you - this valley and these remote and rugged mountains were the Ute Indians' ancestral home way before the white man ever showed his pale face here. Chief Piah sent scouts out weeks ago as soon as the spring thaw started to melt the snow. You would be a fool not to believe they do not already know where you are. I would bet my last coin they are watching us right now."

That statement seemed to make both the 1st Lieutenant and the Master Sergeant nervous as they started scanning the horizon and tree lines as if they were now anticipating an ambush.

The 1st Lieutenant nervously spurred his horse closer to me, speaking with a voice loud enough to try and be an indication that it was he that was in command and not the Master Sergeant, "If you will not tell us where the renegades are, maybe your 'squaw' will?"

I pulled my Colt 44 pistol with lightning speed and pointed it at the little 170 pound weasel with short blond hair and a few sparse blonde whiskers that the U.S. Cavalry called a 1st Lieutenant. Chance, with more speed than I, also palmed his Colt 44 and pointed it at Master Sergeant Andy Cacy. Kellie Shawn and Walk With Ghost, also showing no fear, had swiftly pulled their Winchester rifles from their saddle scabbards and had them pointed in the direction of the rest of the U.S. Calvary troopers. Mutt, the half wolf and half something else dog, even crouched into an attack position.

Master Sergeant Andy Cacy with a smile and no fear simply said, "Fastest damn pistol draws I have ever seen."

1st Lieutenant Wilson's eyes were blinking fast as he tried to regain his composure as I pointed the killing end of my Colt pistol at his noggin. I let him sweat for a few seconds before I spoke, "Since I get the feeling you are new to the Rocky Mountain frontier, let there be no misunderstanding. You said 'squaw' like she was less than human, and I take offense to that. Walk With Ghost is her name, and she is a princess of the Ute Indian Nation and a member of the Grand River Ute tribe. Her brother and my brother-in-law is named Chief Piah. You will treat my wife with the respect that any woman of her stature deserves, or you will answer to me, Matt Lee."

The Master Sergeant's eyes grew larger at the mention of my name. Thinking while I still had the 1st Lieutenant's attention I spoke again, "And before either of you make another foolish mistake, I should inform both of you that before you go calling the other woman a greaser or some other foul name, her name is Kellie Shawn Arriaga and she is the sister of a well-known bandit in Mexico named Chucho el Roto and she happens to be the lady love of my friend Chance Bondurant."

Master Sergeant Andy Cacy with an even broader smile, slapped his leg as he said, "I will be damned! Chance Bondurant and Matt Lee!"

1st Lieutenant Wilson was not pleased at his Master Sergeant's reaction and the fact that I still had my Colt pointed between his eyes. He tried to draw on what little courage he had, but his voice cracked as the fear won out, "You won't shoot me; my troopers would cut you down. You would not survive the ordeal."

Smiling as I spoke, "You and your troopers are green as grass and the only one with any sand and battle experience at all here is your Master Sergeant. I would say it would just be even odds if it came to shooting against the four of us. And if I was a betting man, I would bet on us. Regardless of the outcome 1st Lieutenant Wilson, you would be the first one standing in line at the pearly gates."

Laughing out loud now, Master Sergeant Cacy in a joyful manner said, "Matt Lee, you are correct. The 1st Lieutenant is a new arrival in the Colorado Territory. Hot damn! Lieutenant, you best say you are sorry and damn well mean it. Matt Lee, who the Indians call "Ghost" is one of the most famous men in the Rocky Mountain frontier. By God, he fought the whole Ute Indian nation to a standstill years back by himself and now he is an honored warrior amongst their tribe. And the other fellow is Chance Bondurant, who just last autumn tracked down and single-handedly killed all but one of the Biggers and Hammond gang. Hell, I think they both are kin to the famous gunfighter Lucas Eldridge down in Central City. Yes Sir 1st Lieutenant, if I was you I would sure as hell tell that man you are sorry."

Sweat droplets, despite the cool spring air, started to form on the forehead of the 1st Lieutenant as he tried to ponder his way out of not looking like a fool in front of his men and not getting his head plowed by a 44 slug. After several seconds as the tension mounted, the 1st Lieutenant cleared his voice and spoke in a slow but even manner, "Being new to the area Mr. Lee, I was not accustomed to the term 'squaw' being a derogatory word, and I would hope your wife would accept my apology."

With my pistol still pointed at the Lieutenant's head and never taking my eye off of him, "What do you think Walk With Ghost? Do you accept this man's apology?"

Walk With Ghost in perfect English and still pointing her Winchester in the direction of the still mounted troopers replied, "I think he sounded sincere enough. Yes, I accept his apology."

As I holstered my Colt 44, Chance did the same and the women put their rifles back in their saddle scabbards. 1st Lieutenant Wilson was so relieved he almost fainted and about fell out of his saddle. Master Sergeant Cacy when he saw this rolled his eyes in disgust.

Dismissing the 1st Lieutenant from my thoughts, I turned toward the Master Sergeant and replied, "If and when you find the Ute Indian camp, you will also find the body of the last outlaw Rick Alvardo of the Biggers and Hammond gang. As for being kin, Lucas Eldridge, Chance Bondurant, and I are not blood related in any way, but I assure you that we all are cut from the same cloth."

Still with that big smile the Master Sergeant spoke, "I reckon so, Matt Lee, I reckon so."

CHAPTER 2

R iding up closer so I could speak to the Master Sergeant and completely dismissing the 1st Lieutenant as if he was not even there, "Would you like some friendly advice son?"

Pointing to his troopers yonder who were almost to a man still boys and wet behind the ears, "If and when you find the Ute renegades, I would plan on talking them into going to the reservation, and I mean you not that piece of crap 1st Lieutenant.

Chief Piah, after 30 seconds with that man, would sooner slit him from crotch to eyeball with a dull eagle bone. I know the man better than most. The chief realizes that the Ute way of life in these mountains is vanishing like the melting snow, and this last winter was his way of spitting in the eye of the U.S. government, sort of his last hurrah. The chief realizes his fate and that of his people is now in the hands of the "Great Spirit" and he feels that his people's only peace and salvation is probably on that reservation out in Utah territory. He is a good man with a true heart and does not want to see his people hurt or killed, but I warn you if you fight him, you will lose. His warriors are battle hardened and fierce and would like nothing more than to spill the blood of the young green as grass troopers out there. That's my advice, so take it or leave it; all I ask you is to roll it around some and not be too hasty to draw your pistol or saber."

Master Sergeant Cacy, looking me in the eye, "I will take it in under advisement sir. I wish to see these youngsters home safe as well."

I reached out and shook the hand of the Master Sergeant and before giving my mare Spirit her head and some rein, I looked at 1st Lieutenant Wilson one last time, and he cowered from my glance and could not look me in the eye. This one was weak and would only get those boys killed; I would never understand why the army puts such men in command positions just because they had a tad more schooling than others. White man thinking always baffled me; with the Indians it was always cut and dried and one did not have to guess what they were discerning.

Without speaking, I nodded toward Chance to indicate we were done here. Mutt, the half wolf and half something else dog, took the point moving south in between the dark timber and aspen trees with Bondurant following then Kellie Shawn. As Walk With Ghost passed me, she reached out and lovingly touched my hand and smiled.

Moving my mare Spirit in behind my wife and her pinto mare named Sky, I could not help but think how much I loved that woman even after 30 plus years of being together. And as we moved further away from the troopers, a smile slowly appeared as I watched the swaying motion of Walk With Ghost's backside as she rode in front of me. Even in her 50 plus years, she was still a beautiful woman that still took my breath away when I watched her undress. Walk With Ghost's hair was coal black with several streaks of gray intermixed into her two braids that reached to the middle of her back. She was a small woman, but living in the Rocky Mountain frontier all her life had made her as strong as any man I knew. The term frail would never be a word anyone would use to describe her. Her face is thin and soft and does not have the sharpness and hard look like that of so many Ute Indian women. Her eyes of course were the color of the acorns that fall from the trees.

When we stand side by side, even though we were roughly the same age, most folks would think she is a lot younger than I. Living the adventurous life in the Rocky Mountains has taken its toll on my body. Although my body is still strong on my 6'2" burly frame, I feel my age, especially in the morning when I try to get my muscles loosened up to start the day. The aches and pains of rugged mountain life are with me mostly in the morning after sleeping. Of course being shot five times and stabbed twice doesn't help matters much. Age has turned my shoulder length hair white and my short beard gray. I tell Walk With Ghost it is the high mountain air that turned my hair this color and she laughs every time and says, "No my love, you are just getting old." My eyes are brown and Walk With Ghost tells me they look like those of a beautiful woman - not a description I am proud of, but it sure does sound nice when she says it to me.

As we rode south toward the settlement of Grand Lake, I was enjoying the spring weather here in the Kawuneeche Valley. The aspens had not started to bud yet and there was still plenty of snow as we followed the trail. Spring always comes later at these higher altitudes than it does down below in places like Denver. I looked at the never summer mountains that never lose the snow from their white tipped peaks and from past experiences knew that in these high and remote mountains, they can create their own weather patterns in the downdraft and updraft of air that flowed over them, which can make snow or rain in any month of the year. It was dangerous for those not prepared for the sudden changes in the weather up so high. This territory called Colorado was where I chose to live and with the Lord as my witness, I knew in my heart it was the most beautiful and wondrous place on earth.

We rode in silence as all of those in tune with the mountains and nature around them did, listening to the music of the Rockies such as the mountain bluebird that just started to sing its song of happiness. The chilled wind rustled the evergreen needles that Chance called the "tree whispers" which seemed like a fitting name to me. My senses were also tuned into the sounds of hazards in the mountains, and make no mistake there was danger in all the beauty that surrounded me, be it a pissed off grizzly bear or mountain lion or it could be as simple as a slip on a small rock while you were walking that breaks a leg.

Above my head was a red-tailed hawk starting its spring courtship in an ever widening circle as it tried to entice a lady red-tailed hawk. If you were lucky to survive the hard winter of ice and snow, spring was the time of year to start fresh and new. It was just as true for man as it was for all the mountain critters.

By mid-afternoon we had found a suitable place to camp for the night that was surrounded by evergreen trees that would offer plenty of protection from the wind and the snow. It would also provide us enough drinking water once melted on the campfire.

As I saw to the four horses - my mare Spirit, Walk With Ghost's pinto Sky, Kellie Shawn's mare Strawberry and of course Chance's mare Storm - I watched the others as they started to set up camp for the night.

I watched Chance Bondurant and Kellie Shawn Arriaga as they seemed to work as one person without much speaking or fanfare. It was obvious they were very much in love and were meant for one another.

Chance and Kellie Shawn had become a couple after he had trailed her last autumn to the Ute renegade camp after she had been kidnapped by the outlaw Rick Alvardo of the Biggers and Hammond gang.

Chance I knew from before when I helped mentor him some in his youth and taught him the way of the gun and the mountains when he was living with my best friend, the famous righteous gunfighter Lucas Eldridge and his wife Devon.

After learning from the best, Chance then went on the vengeance trail for justice when a roaming outlaw gang had killed his younger brother. In the autumn of last year, young Chance left the bodies of the entire Biggers and Hammond gang strung out through the towns and settlements of the Rockies until the last remaining outlaw Alvardo, who was a half Ute Indian and half Mexican, had ended up in the Ute renegade camp. Of course in the custom of the Ute warriors, Chance and Alvardo fought a death match, which of course Chance came out the victor after almost dying himself.

It made me proud to know that I helped some in the upbringing and schooling of Chance in the way of the mountains and how to fight and live the life as a warrior. Chance was as tall as I was but with a tad more muscle on his frame. His hair and eyes were brown and Walk With Ghost said he was a mighty handsome fellow; I saw nothing that would dispute that. After Walk With Ghost and I had lost our two sons early in life to this rugged life on the mountain frontier, Chance Bondurant became - if not in blood, but in my heart - my son.

Kellie Shawn Arriaga was Mexican and was a sister of a famous bandit in Mexico. She was about the same size as Walk With Ghost and a stunning beauty on top of that. Her eyes of blue with a hint of green were an unusual color for a Mexican woman, and her hair was dark as coal, worn in a single braid that ended in the middle of her back. She was like most Mexican women that I had known with a fiery demeanor about her. One thing that was true about Kellie Shawn was that she loved her man like no other.

After a filling supper of some venison, beans, and campfire tortillas that we had brought with us from the Ute Indian encampment and with the sun settling down behind the mountains to the west, we rolled out our bedrolls for the evening. We would sleep easy tonight because we could count on the half wolf and half something else Mutt to give us advance warning of any danger that might present itself.

Using my saddle as a pillow and my Colt pistol under the saddle and Winchester close by in case I needed it in a hurry, I felt Walk With Ghost cuddle up to me under the buffalo robe. We watched in silence as the stars twinkled and danced in the sky on this almost full moon night. In the distance we could hear the howl of a lonesome wolf. Walk With Ghost drifted off to sleep and I watched her for several minutes and thanked the Lord for having her grace my life before I went to sleep myself.

CHAPTER 3

After a stunning dark orange sunrise in a cloudless heaven the next morning, our breakfast was the same as our supper the night before of venison, beans, and campfire tortillas.

Mutt the half wolf did, however, supply some entertainment as he tried unsuccessfully to capture a chipmunk for his own breakfast. The chipmunk dashed from an evergreen tree to another tree running up the trunk each time just an inch or so higher than Mutt's ability to jump. Then just as Mutt gave up the chase, the chipmunk once again would scamper to the ground and face Mutt as if to challenge him, which started the cycle all over again. Mutt finally gave up the pursuit and it seemed almost as if he was embarrassed as Chance fed him some venison steak. Walk With

Ghost and Kellie Shawn were still smiling about this morning escapade with the half wolf and the chipmunk as we started back on the trail toward Grand Lake.

The snow on the trail we were following was already broken by the troop of the U.S. Calvary that we had seen the following day as they headed in the opposite direction searching for Chief Piah and his renegade Ute Indians. I was bothered by the fact that the Troopers had undoubtedly bivouacked in or near the settlement of Grand Lake, which told me there were certainly more soldiers in the area. There was no question that the U.S. government looked upon Chief Piah and the others as a hostile threat to the Rocky Mountain frontier.

Chief Piah knew full well his refusal to go onto the reservation might have deadly consequences for him and his renegades. One of the reasons I needed to get Walk With Ghost away from the Kawuneeche Valley and the Middle Park high mountain plateau region where tensions would be running high this early spring was to teach her how to deal with the Ute Indians to see if they were friendly or not.

It had been my experience that most white people were scared of the Indians only because they did not understand how they lived and how they thought. I admit the differences between the white folks and the Indians were vast, and it is a sad tale indeed that most whites did not have the ability to recognize, accept, and celebrate those differences, which was what was causing all the pain and suffering on both sides of the issue.

On the same hand though, the Ute Indians - just like the plains Indians - were finding it difficult and it most cases refused to accept the inevitable fate that their way of life was fast disappearing. The continuous flow of white townsfolks, settlers, miners, and ranchers was something that could not be stopped. The Indian mind could not fathom how many white people there really were; they had no concept of expansion and exploration.

All these things and hatred toward the Indian were out of my hands and beyond my control. All I wanted was a place in the high mountains where Walk With Ghost and I could live out our days in relative peace and harmony. Looking toward the heavens and the Lord, I thought to myself, "That really is not that much to ask for."

A crow, a very big black crow, disrupted my thinking as it landed in the evergreen tree just ahead of me. It seemed to be watching me and only me. Gently pulling back on Spirit's reins, I brought her to a halt as I studied the crow as it studied me. Crows like this one are a mystic animal to the Ute Indians. They were believed to know all the mysteries in life and were able to foretell the future. They also were a symbol of impending death, which is why I stopped to study this crow. The others had not seen it land since they were all ahead of me on the trail and having lived among the Ute Indians long enough, I did not dismiss their beliefs and I pondered why this crow chose to let only me see it.

After several minutes I decided to press on but could feel the eyes of the crow follow me as I rode Spirit to pass it. It gave me a sense of dread and premonition.

Trying to put the ill feeling that the crow had given me in the back of my mind, I tried to think of our final destination today and that was Grand Lake.

Grand Lake had become the main outfitting and supply point for the mining camps of Lulu City, Teller City, and Gaskill in the more rugged mountains that surrounded the Kawuneeche Valley. The settlement was set on the shores of what is one of the most alluring lakes in the high country of Colorado. The lake was said to be over 300 feet deep and crystal clear, so clear in fact, you could see all the way to the bottom. Grand Lake was also set at the far northern tip of the Middle Park Basin, which was a flat high mountain plateau surrounded by snowcapped mountains no matter which direction you looked.

Walk With Ghost's and my plan was to travel with Chance and Kellie Shawn until we would split up a day's ride south of Grand Lake when Chance and Kellie Shawn headed west towards Hot Sulphur Springs to finish the task of finding land for her brother's ranch. She had been kidnapped and her bodyguards had been killed last autumn there in Hot Sulfur Springs by Rick Alvardo and two other outlaws. Chance killed the others in a fierce gunfight and trailed Alvardo to the eventual rescue of Kellie Shawn and the final death match with Alvardo at the Ute renegade camp.

My plan was simple enough and that was to get Walk With Ghost far away from this area where tensions would be at an all-time high with the Ute Indians. We were heading south to a hidden valley I knew of not far from Como, Colorado just below the summit of Boreas Pass that we had started to call Redemption Valley. I trapped that area many years ago and had the makings of a good cabin already started there. It was a place we could live far from those that may want to make trouble for us. It was a place we could call home and live our life in amity.

By mid-afternoon we topped out on a small rise just north of Grand Lake, and we were able to watch the settlement below for a spell to get a feeling for what we might encounter when we entered the town. Seeing nothing amiss, we spurred our horses forward.

I let Chance take point as we headed into Grand Lake as he knew the town better than I. Last autumn right here, he fought and killed Herman Biggers, the leader of the Biggers and Hammond gang as he trailed those that had murdered his brother Jace.

Originally I had wanted Walk With Ghost and myself to camp just outside of Grand Lake, but Chance had talked me into staying at the Baldwin Hotel. During his stay last autumn, he had made friends of the owners Sherol Roy and Roger Baldwin and spoke highly of them. I had to admit that Walk With Ghost, after living in a teepee all winter, would probably enjoy a hot bath in a cast iron tub. Chance had assured me that there would be no issues that Walk With Ghost was an Indian with his friends.

Both Chance and I slipped the leather thongs off the hammers of our Colt pistols that kept them safely in our holsters as we rode. Being the cautious men that we were, we wanted to be ready to meet head on any trouble that might present itself in this settlement. Grand Lake was like any other such type of town in the Rocky Mountains and the Colorado Territory and was full of miners, cowboys, freighters, shop keepers, soiled doves and of course malcontents. All that was good and all that was bad of the human race would be present here.

As we entered from the west and rode down the main street of Grand Lake, every man, woman, and child stopped to watch us as we passed them. Thinking about this reaction, I sort of chuckled to myself as I thought of the sight we must have made - a half wolf and half something else dog, an Indian woman, a Mexican woman, a known gunfighter, and a grizzled ole' mountain man. Hell, it would not have been any better if a circus had showed up here in town.

The settlement was busy today, but what caught my eye when we passed one of the saloons was that out front tied to a hitching rail were five horses with the words U.S. Calvary branded on their left hips. I did not see any soldier blue and yellow and could only assume that the troopers were inside having a drink. My gut was telling me this was a bad omen and remembering the crow from earlier, I knew deep down this was not a good sign, not a good sign at all.

After leaving our horses at the livery stable in the care of a man named Howard Smith, who seemed to be on friendly terms with Chance, we made our way to the Baldwin Hotel.

The Baldwin Hotel, just like almost every building in Grand Lake, was built from lodge pole pines and was a simple one floor cabin affair with six rooms and a large covered front porch.

We stepped up onto the front porch as the night finally took hold and the sun disappeared behind the western mountains with the stars starting their nightly dance across the sky.

The owners Roger Baldwin and his wife Sherol Roy happened to be sipping coffee as they sat out on the front porch; it was like a homecoming of sorts as they were plumb happy to see Chance and Mutt. With more than enough smiles to go around, Chance introduced us all and Sherol Roy hugged Chance, Mutt, and myself and gave both Kellie Shawn and Walk With Ghost an extra-long hug. Any thought of Walk With Ghost not being accepted at the Baldwin Hotel was soon forgotten.

Roger was an older man of medium height and build with gray hair and a white goatee and he wore a tied down Colt pistol. His wife Sherol Roy was small and a pleasant enough woman with short graying hair and a smile as big as the whole outdoors. It was obvious that Mutt and Sherol Roy were pals as he seemed to take a shine to her as he trotted right up to her and rolled over on his back for a belly rub, which Sherol Roy was more than happy to oblige him.

After checking us in and showing us our rooms, Sherol Roy started to fix us some supper and since at this moment in time we were the only guests, it was like being with kin; Kellie Shawn and

Walk With Ghost pitched in and helped Sherol Roy prepare a supper of elk stew, fried taters, and Dutch oven biscuits.

Over the course of supper, Roger was curious about what had happened to Chance after he left last autumn in search of the outlaw Alvardo and subsequent rescue of Kellie Shawn. Chance, not accustomed to being the focus of attention, quickly told his and Kellie Shawn's story without much fanfare, keeping it pretty low keyed. Roger knew there was much more to the story, but out of respect for his friend Chance did not press it any further.

Roger then turned his attention to me, "Matt Lee, you are one of the most famous men in the Rocky Mountains and everyone has heard the tales about you, but one thing I have never heard talked about is why the Ute Indians call you "Ghost."

Chance, who was more than happy to have someone else the topic of conversation, added, "You know Matt Lee, that is a story I would like to hear also. Why do they call you Ghost?"

I was going to decline except for Walk With Ghost reached over and patted my forearm and said, "Tell them Ghost, these are your friends and they should hear you tell the tale."

CHAPTER 4

L ooking at Walk With Ghost, I could never ever deny her when she smiled at me like this. The tale of my naming by the Utes was never something I spoke of. I was ashamed of who I was in those days; when one's mind snaps and you go mad, it is nothing to be proud of. I tried to forget those days that had turned into months, then years, but most nights I relive them in my dreams. Maybe speaking of them now would help ease the pain of those times.

I looked around the table and those that sat there: Chance Bondurant, who in my heart I knew as my son was a man I was proud to say I helped in some of his upbringing; Kellie Shawn Arriaga was a woman whom I had grown to love like a daughter this last winter, and she had become dear friends with Walk With

Ghost and myself; and Sherol Roy and Roger Baldwin whom I had only known this day and evening, but I could feel their goodness and their true heart because it radiated from them for all to see.

My eyes finally settled on Walk With Ghost, the woman whom I have loved all these years and who loved me unconditionally when I would wander far from home. It seemed she understood why I had to wander more than I understood it myself. I did not deserve her love, but she loved me nonetheless. In my wanderings I always loved her, never stopped loving her, and will always and forever love her until the day I die. And if there is life after this one, I will love her once again. Fate and the Lord smiled once again on me the day Walk With Ghost entered my life. My mind cleared, the insanity left, and my heart was filled with caring and not hatred anymore. Walk With Ghost saved my sanity, heart, and my life.

Walk With Ghost tilted her head in a manner I knew so well; she already knew the thoughts that were spoken in my head and with love in her voice, "Maybe it is time Ghost to speak of those times once again."

I cleared my voice and it was not long before I was lost once again in my past. "I guess I should start off with what I learned so many years ago. One should always hold and care for the love in your heart; as soon as you lose that you walk the edge of insanity, and only a slight push to one side can make you drop over into madness. This I know to be true.

As a young man and still green as grass, I decided to become a mountain man and try my luck in the fur trade of those times. I went to work for two men named William Bent and Ceran St. Vrain, who had established Bent's Fort almost 300 miles south of here on the Arkansas River.

While learning the craft of trapping and skinning of wild critters, I met four other trappers about my age and like myself full of piss and vinegar that would become like brothers to me. Dan Buxman was a tall and lanky fellow that hailed from the Smokey Mountains out east; Mike Sands was a quiet and shy boy that was a hard worker and never complained; Jay Edwards was a redhead that was the fastest skinner of critters that I had to this day ever seen; and of course Sam Walter who was another redhead who said he played many musical instruments, which I had no doubt because he carried and played the mouth harp that some call a harmonica so beautifully that we all would stop what we were doing to listen to him. I never admitted it to the others, but sometimes I was moved to tears by Sam's music. We became friends, good friends and brothers until the end.

After a season of trapping and working together, we all thought of ourselves as wealthy, or as wealthy as a mountain man could become in those days working for others. We all owned two horses, one for riding and one for packing pelts. Each of us had the tools to be a mountain man such as a riding saddle, a bridle, six to eight beaver traps each, a small wooden box that carried beaver bait, tobacco kit, powder horn, bullet pouch, a hatchet or battle ax, butcher knife, two pairs of deerskin moccasins, a fire starter kit that had tender and flint, a coat made of buffalo robes, leather antelope breeches, one wool and one flannel shirt, and caps made of otter or fox. After the first year of trapping, we had all made enough money to sell our Pennsylvania or Kentucky rifles and purchase at twice the cost the "new" percussion cap 50 caliber Hawkins. We were young and in our eyes wealthy and indestructible.

We were happy and living the life that we all believed we were meant to live in the high never summer mountains under the forever skies. That all changed one spring when we met an older man that walked the mountains of old before us. His name was Tom Driscoll; he didn't tell us much about himself that I can remember, but what still sticks in my mind was his tale of Spanish gold and a cave. This tale, his story of the lost cave of gold, would change my life - forever.

The old mountain man Tom Driscoll told us of the legendary La Caverna Del Oro which in Spanish means the cave of gold, which was 150 miles due west of Bents Fort in the Sangre de Cristo Mountains which means "Blood Of Christ" in Spanish.

Stopping the tale for a minute while I sipped some water, I could tell everyone present was fascinated and waited patiently for me to continue. I was caught up in my tale of my own story; it was as if I was reliving it as I spoke. Walk With Ghost patted my arm lovingly as I continued, "Driscoll told us around the campfire that evening that in the mid 1500's, three monks from the Spanish Coronado expedition, while exploring the Sangre de Cristo

Mountains for gold, had heard a tale told by some Indians about a mysterious cave protected by demons high up on the mountain. Intrigued the monks, doing what monks did during those days to pagans, enslaved the Indians and forced them to locate the cave. Upon discovery of the cave, the monks also found what they were truly looking for and that was gold - gold and riches beyond belief. The monks made the enslaved Indians by force dig the gold from the cave. The cave being located high above timberline could only be mined in the summer months due to heavy snow during the winter. So the Spanish whipped and beat their slave Indians to try and get them to work faster and harder.

After being enslaved and beaten by the Spanish monks for that long summer, the Indians revolted and attacked the heavily armed Spanish and all the Indians were killed except one who had escaped to tell the story of what had happened at the demon cave high up on the mountain.

During the Indian slave revolt, the Indians inflicted some heavy damage on the Spanish and killed two of the monks. The remaining monk whose name was De La Cruz and the surviving members of the expedition packed the gold on their pack animals, which was in those days a vast amount of gold and returned southward to Mexico before the cold and snow of the harsh mountain winter came blowing down from the north.

The Spanish never returned to La Caverna Del Oro. Driscoll said that De La Cruz, the only surviving monk of the ill-fated expedition, was the only one who knew the exact location of the demon gold, but he caught a fever upon his return to Mexico and died. Driscoll thought maybe the monk had taken the demon back with him or maybe it was justice in the end that prevailed.

The ancestors of the Ute Indians were said to have never returned to the depths of La Caverna Del Oro as they thought of it as the demon cave where so much pain and suffering had been inflicted upon their loved ones. Others believed that the Indians now protect the mountain after being directed by their Great Spirit to stop anyone from ever stepping foot in the cave again.

Tom Driscoll also added to the story that for all white men down through the years, the location of the cave of riches had been forgotten, but never the tale of La Caverna Del Oro.

Driscoll told us that he never had the courage himself to look for the cave of gold, but he loved the story and retelling the legend.

The next morning after the old man told us of the legend, he simply walked back into the wilderness, never to be seen again. Since the five of us were young and adventurous and at the time had the means to do so, we all decided half-heartedly and with a laugh that we would band together to look for the cave and the gold. At the time we did not realize what a foolish thought it was.

CHAPTER 5

A fter a small break so all of us could eat some mincemeat pie that Sherol Roy had served up, I continued with the tale of my past. It almost felt good to talk about it after all these years and after clearing my throat, I began again, "That morning that Tom Driscoll had faded into the wilderness, the five of us began to talk at length and with more seriousness about going to find the La Caverna Del Oro. It was an adventure for the young and as it turned out, for the not so very bright.

That morning during breakfast, we all began to recall the clues that Driscoll had laid out in his tale about the location of the cave of gold. We knew it was roughly 150 miles west of us in the Spanish Peaks region and supposedly on the newly named Marble Mountain. After making a pact, the five of us decided to give it one summer to look for the lost cave and to see if the legend was true.

After deciding that was what we were going to do, we wasted no time in informing our employers William Bent and Ceran St. Vrain we would be leaving. And with a halfhearted laugh, we told them we would be back for trapping season penniless and broke looking for work. They assured us we would be welcomed back with open arms.

Being used to having to pack our mounts in a hurry, we were able to head west and into the unknown about midday. We were jovial and in high-spirits; it was good to be on such an adventure with those that could easily be your brothers.

All I recall about the trip to Marble Mountain was that it went well and after about eight days or so, we found ourselves camping at the base of Marble Mountain. The country and the lay of the land were new to us, but it was still the Rocky Mountains and all five of us lived and breathed the Rockies.

From our vantage point as we rode from the east, we could tell that the top of Marble Mountain was well above where the trees never grew anymore, possibly 3,000 feet or more above timberline. According to the tale as it was told by old man Driscoll, the cave of gold was located just above timberline and on the southwest side of the face of the mountain. With no other clue to go by and all of us knowing this was probably a folly and a one in a million chance, we were nonetheless game and ready for the adventure. We headed to the southwest side of Marble Mountain.

It was on the third or fourth day of exploring the southwest side that I started to see the crows - never more than one at a time and I was never sure if it was the same crow or not - but it or they seemed to be watching us. I brought it up to the others at supper, and they laughed at me and kidded me for being scared of my own shadow. Of course I laughed it off also with my friends, but when Sam began to play his harmonica that evening, I could not shake the feeling that we were being watched from close and afar. I had difficulty sleeping that night because the sounds of the woods and timber were different. I could not put my finger on it, but the sounds of the wilderness had changed. I kept my new Hawkins rifle close and the powder under the buffalo robe I used for sleeping to keep it dry. My gut instinct was telling me something was off kilter in the woods that surrounded us.

The next morning after some dried venison jerky for breakfast, we set out again to explore. Mike Sands saw it first and yelled for all of us to come running. What he discovered was an ancient fortress at the mouth of a small cave. And I mean ancient like 300 years before ancient. The walls of the fort were constructed of rock and timbers, and rifle pits had been constructed for its defense, which led all five of us to suspect that Driscoll's story of the Spanish legend and the three monks was in fact a true telling of an antique but not forgotten story.

Dan Buxman found an old tarnished brass Spanish helmet and breastplate and handed the breast plate to me with a huge grin. I could not help but notice it had a hole in it roughly where the person's heart would have been.

Since the ancient fort we found was just below timberline and according to the tale told by the old man Driscoll the La Caverna Del Oro was above timber line, we set out to explore above the old fort. Once again a crow or "the" crow landed in an evergreen directly in front of me and watched me as I rode by him. Now looking back after all these years, I now know it was a warning and I did not have the wherewithal to understand it then. With an odd feeling of dread, I continued on and upwards with my friends.

Within a couple of hours Jay Edwards had found the entrance to a much larger cave. As we all bunched up to check out the cave, we were excited and more than positive it was La Caverna Del Oro - the Spanish lost cave of gold. There was a faded but apparent red Maltese cross marking the entrance to the cave. We were all dumbfounded, for we had known there was a small chance of ever finding the cave, but here we were and destiny had led us straight to it.

We were obviously jovial, laughing and punching each other in the arms about our find, but since it was well past midday and we were all hungry, we decided to make camp at the entrance and fry up some venison steaks and beans from our supplies. The others spoke of what they would do with our newly found riches even though we actually had not found any gold yet. I was quiet and reserved; the feeling of dread was overpowering me and I kept my eyes on the tree lines surrounding our camp. We had tied our horses and pack horses to a picket line in between two trees and I kept an eye on them also.

After a filling supper of venison steak, Sam Walters broke out his harmonica and started to play a merry tune. I attempted to join in the festivities of the moment, but I failed as I remembered something the old man Tom Driscoll had said and we all had seemed to forget, "Others believe that the Indians now protect the mountain and the demon cave after being directed by their "Great Spirit" to stop anyone from ever stepping foot in the cave again."

Remembering this part of the tale, I felt that overwhelming sense of foreboding again and decided to bring it up to the others as soon as Sam's merry rendition on his harmonica was over.

Which, as it turned out, was sooner than ole' Sam and the rest of us ever imagined as an arrow pierced his throat dead center of his arms as they were raised holding and playing his harmonica. The remaining four of us were slow in moving as we were all in some sort of shock momentarily as we watched Sam gurgle on his own blood and paw at the killing arrow in his throat.

The next to go down was Dan Buxman as more Indians than I could count stormed our small encampment; Dan took a lance through the back that pierced him through and through.

Maybe because I had been on edge already because my gut instinct had told me things were off kilter, I had my Hawkins rifle loaded and primed, and I shot and killed the Indian that had killed poor Dan.

Out of the corner of my eye, I saw Jay Edwards taken off his feet as two of the wild Injuns tackled him; he really never had a chance as they went to work on him with their killing tomahawks.

Mike Sands and I were also attacked by numerous hostiles and we were giving them all they wanted with our tomahawks and skinning knives. In the initial onslaught I had cut and cleaved two, and Mike had taken down three as we fought for our lives in front of the La Caverna Del Oro.

We had a few moments to catch our breaths after the first rush of hostiles, and as we looked at each other knowing this was our day to die, we nodded at each other as only friends can do in the face of certain death. Death awaited us and as true warriors, we knew that we were not going to make it easy for those that wanted us dead. Taking my weapons and swinging my arms back in forth in front of me to limber up, I was ready and even willing as the next wave of hostiles rushed in at us.

Covered in blood and not really knowing if it was ours or theirs and with our Hawkins now useless and forgotten in the battle, we fought like savages and madmen slashing and hammering with our skinning knives and tomahawks. I lost count of how many Indians we either killed or had maimed in those moments of blood lust and at the height of the battle in front of the demon cave. All the while during the blood, killing, and slaughter, we were being pushed back closer and closer to the entrance to the cave.

I saw Mike go down to one knee as one of the hostiles was able to hit him at the top of his shoulder with a tomahawk. Seeing my friend Mike and brother still fighting from this now almost defenseless position, I fought and killed my way to his side and was able to grab him and lift him back to his feet. Out of the corner of my eye I saw the darkness of the cave and I grabbed Mike and rushed headlong into the darkness and the entrance of the La Caverna Del Oro."

CHAPTER 6

During the telling of my tale, I and everyone else had lost track of time and the night hours grew long. I asked if they would like me to finish in the morning and all of them responded at the exact same time - No. They all were caught up in the story as I was. Chance was the one who spoke as he was twirling his hand in a "get on with it" motion, "You can't stop now Matt Lee; I know you better than anyone here except Walk With Ghost and I had no idea. I would never be able to sleep without hearing the rest of the story."

Taking another sip of water and clearing my voice once again, images of what happened that day flooded my mind again as I started to speak, "Once Mike and I entered the cave, I thought we maybe had a few more minutes to live; the battle so far had sapped my strength and my muscles were starting to waver. I didn't have much left to fight with and looking at my friend Mike and his shoulder as the blood flowed out of his wound as he was slumped against me, I knew he had even less.

Slowly lowering Mike to the ground in a sitting position, I handed him his weapons he had dropped so he could maybe get one more hostile. Mike gritted his teeth and readied himself as best he could as he looked at me. His eyes seemed hollow and his face had grown pale from the blood loss, but he was still ready to go out fighting like the warrior I knew him to be. After getting Mike my friend ready for the last and final battle, I turned back toward the entrance to ready myself for the last hurrah. Swinging my arms once again to limber myself up - I waited - and nothing.

Standing in silence, I could see out the entrance and the hostile Indians were still there, but not advancing. Hell, they even looked as if they were scared shitless. I sure enough was baffled; the hostile Indians had lost many of their warriors in their attack on us. Mike and I were frazzled and done in and would and could not pose much of a challenge anymore. Not fifteen feet separated the hostile Indians from where I stood inside the cave, but they did not advance.

Mike always had more meat in his brain pan than I and realizing it first, he started to laugh, not a chuckle but a full-fledged belly laugh, "Hell, Matt Lee they are scared."

Total confusion fogged my brain as I watched the Indians just outside. Hell, I could have spit on them if I had enough moisture to form a spit, "Scared? Of us?"

Grimacing with pain, but still with a huge smile, "No, not 'us' you big dummy. Those savages are scared of the cave or demons and the haunted legend. We are safe as long as we are in here." Realizing Mike was right, I started to laugh, "If that don't beat all, those barbarians are scared of the dark."

Looking out, I could see that the day was just about done and within the hour the sun would drop below the western mountain tops.

Knowing we were still dead men looking for a place to lie down and die, I felt some relief in the fact at least we would be able to catch our breath before the specter of death found us. Still alive, but trapped in a cave with only one entrance with six hostile warriors waiting for us just on the outside, it was only a matter of time. We had no food or water and no means of making a fire. Our

Hawkins rifles we had been so proud of had been discarded at the height of the battle as soon as they had been fired and now in the possession of the Indians that wanted us dead. I was just thankful that they had no idea how the Hawkins worked or they could use them to shoot into the cave.

I took inventory of my own body and was surprised that I had actually come through the battle with no real injuries to speak of - a few small cuts and more than a dozen bruises. I decided the best course of action would be to try and get some sleep and rest up and come first light in the morning ready myself for battle once again before I became weak from not eating or having any water.

Mike Sands was a different matter altogether. If he survived the night he was done for and would not be able to fight in the morning or ever. His wound was severe and bleeding and more likely than not he would bleed out before morning.

Walking over to where Mike was, I sat down next to him and I could see the pain and suffering in his eyes as he tried to fight his anguish of knowing he was on the verge of death. Mike looked at me and with pain in his voice, "Matt Lee I am done for - just like the others. Promise me that you will stay with me my friend until I pass. Having these few moments of time to ponder some about it, I don't want to be alone when I die."

Laying Mike's head on my shoulder, I held him and said nothing as the sun fully faded into the night. Holding him and looking out the cave at the bodies of Sam, Dan, and Jay in the flickering campfire the Indians had built, I realized life is meaningless without true friends and nothing else on this earth had more meaning than friendship. I had learned to love these men, these mountain men like no other. I felt proud to be able to share my adventure thus far in life with men such as this. They had been more than friends; they had been my brothers and if it is my fate to die here on this mountain with them, I could think of no better way to die than amongst men of courage and strength. I felt Mike shudder as I held him for the last time as his life seeped away.

Tears formed in my eyes and I started to cry. Crying is good for the soul, but after you get it out of your system, you have to man up and face the reality of the situation. I was not yet ready to face reality and for now I cried for the death of my friends and I cried holding Mike until I had no more tears. Weariness, anguish, and the death of my friends had taken its toll on me and soon I either passed out or just fell asleep.

After I stopped my story for a minute to regain my composure, Walk With Ghost reached out and hugged me. Kellie Shawn and Sherol Roy had tears in their eyes. Roger and Chance had looks of sadness on their faces, and I never felt more vulnerable than I did at that moment. I had opened up and showed everyone here my weakness. I looked at Walk With Ghost and I saw her love for me as she smiled and somehow made me feel better. Clearing my voice from any emotion knowing I had gone this far, I was going all the way and finish the story, "Having lost all concept of time in the dark and distress of the moment, I am not sure how long I had been asleep when I heard the voices - not voices from outside the cave, but voices within the cave. With the voices came a cold wind that came from the vastness from the depths of the cave. How the wind was formed I cannot tell you now other than it was there when it had not been before - and it was real!"

The cold and icy wind made me shiver, and I held my arms tight to my body to try and keep warm, but to no avail. The voices were carried on the wind and it was not long before I realized what I was hearing were memories and sounds from the past and of folks that lived long before I was ever born. I am here to tell you as a man that believes in the "Lord Ole' Mighty" that what I heard and what I saw the remainder of that cold, dark night were ghosts, ancient and some not so ancient ghosts. I knew then that the legend was true - La Caverna Del Oro was haunted.

I shivered from the cold and fear as the voices surrounded me. The haunting voices were in many different languages; some I had heard before like Spanish, French, English, and what I now know is the Ute Indian language. There were countless other languages that to this day I have no knowledge of. The words and voices spoke over one another most of the time, but once in a while they would stop and only one language could be heard.

For a man that had never felt fear and saw himself as fearless, I was scared. And my fear grew more as the visions started – visions in flashes of light. It was as if there was a lightning storm within the walls of the cave with flashes of brilliant blue and yellow light. With each lightning strike of light, I saw men as if I was looking through the rips and slashes in a blanket hung as a doorway between two rooms. I saw the Spanish dressed in armor as they beat and whipped the Indian slaves. I saw in these glimpses of light and time Indians who I now know were the Ute Indians as they revolted against their captors. I saw death; I saw hatred; and I saw the misery that night in La Caverna Del Oro of all things from the ancient past.

With the icy cold wind and the flashes of men long dead, I felt the malevolent that lived there in the cave - evil as I had never felt before and it frightened me. As the wind, long dead voices, ghosts, and the wicked flowed over me, I felt the evil romance me and try to make me one with it. It was at that moment I felt my mind snap. I died a little that night there in the cave and in that malevolent wind amongst the dead and the ghosts. Believe me my friends I have never forgotten it and have pondered the meaning of all that happened that night and for the next two years following.

CHAPTER 7

When talking about one's madness, it makes you seem small and trivial in the world and this is how I felt as I took several sips of water. Not wanting to look into the eyes of my friends and see sympathy for me, because I didn't deserve sympathy, I avoided looking directly at them as I closed my eyes and the memories continued. Turning in the direction of Walk With Ghost, I faced her and only her when I opened my eyes again. Clearing my voice I spoke again, "I truly believe I lost my mind that night after the first battle. As daylight started to flood the entrance of La Caverna Del Oro, the icy wind with the ancient obsessing voices disappeared. I saw no more flashes of light and dead men from the past; even my dear friend had passed on, leaving me alone in the darkness holding on to Mike's very dead and very cold body.

Something had changed deep inside of me; something had turned in my soul. I no longer felt sadness or fear. The only emotion that ran rampant in me was anger. More than anger really, it was… rage. Looking out through the halo of light that was a new day, I counted my enemy again and there still were six of them, and I hated them. I hated them for killing my friends! I hated them for forcing me to spend the night in this godforsaken haunted cave! I hated them for living!

Standing just inches in the darkness, I was safe from attack from the fierce Ute Indian warriors just a few feet out in the light. Even in my rage I could think clearly and I knew to survive leaving this cave, I would need an advantage of some kind.

As if the cave heard or read my thoughts, I saw out of the corner of my eye a golden twinkle flashing near the entrance as the dawn of the new day stretched further into the cave. It was not the gold that the Spanish had enslaved the Indians for, but what that golden twinkle showed me was the location of a long forgotten Spanish brass armor breast plate.

Thinking this was my advantage being shown to me, I scooped it up knowing it would stop any glancing blows from a tomahawk or knife. I tried putting on the breastplate armor over my buckskin shirt, but it was too tight and would restrict my movements when it came to the hand-to-hand combat that would be needed once I walked into the light. I then stripped off my buckskin shirt and wore the Spanish armor next to my naked chest and then put my shirt back on over the armor. Moving my arms here and there, I was not restricted in any way and after clenching my fist and pounding it on the Spanish breast plate and after hearing the hollow sound of the armor, I felt invincible.

Picking up my tomahawk and skinning knife, I once again swung my arms back and forth to limber up my muscles. The Ute Indians in the daylight saw me and knew that soon I was coming out, and they readied themselves to meet me.

Taking one last look at Mike as he lay dead on the floor of the cave, I wondered if the rage I felt inside of me was the so-called demon that the legend spoke of. All I knew in that moment of time is that I wanted to kill those Indians. I was going to make them and any that I ever ran across pay in blood for what happened here on Marble Mountain.

Taking a deep breath to fill my lungs, I was more than ready to bring the battle back to the hostiles, and I moved with swiftness toward the light and the entrance of the cave.

As soon as I stepped into the light, two arrows struck me in the chest and embedded into the armor breast plate. I could feel the arrow tips draw blood as they were stuck in the Spanish armor. The killing end of the arrowheads scratched the surface of my skin; the breast plate had at least temporarily saved my life.

The first warrior came at me with a lance with eagle feathers tied behind the killing point. He lunged the lance at me as I stepped to the right making the lance miss. His miss and forward momentum brought him close to me and with two quick movements I cleaved him in the shoulder with my tomahawk and then took my skinning knife and sliced his throat. Sprayed with the warrior's blood, I turned quickly to meet two more of the Ute Indian warriors as they moved with quickness toward me.

I feared nothing this day since I was filled with rage; on this day and in this battle I knew I was immortal and nothing could harm me. I know it sounds crazy, but I knew it to be true. After killing the warrior with the lance, I knew right there I was going to survive this day. I did not know it at the time, but the Ute legend of "Ghost" was born out of this battle and out of this rage.

The next two were more cautious in their movements and soon were joined by a third Indian and all three were armed as I was armed with one tomahawk each and a knife in their other hand. The first one on my right and the fastest of the three I killed with one blow of my tomahawk to the top of his head. Bloody and dead on his feet, he dropped heavily to the ground. The middle warrior got in close and barely missed my noggin with a powerful swing of his tomahawk which threw him off balance and in turn exposed the side of his throat as he spun to his left. I stabbed once and hard in his exposed throat with my skinning knife, severing any and all of the rivers that flowed blood to his brain. Pulling my knife out of his throat, I watched him fall dead in such a manner that caused the third Indian to stumble over him, and I cleaved him with my tomahawk in the back of his head killing him as instantly as the other two.

Washed with sticky blood and none of it my own, I turned towards the two remaining Ute warriors who were staring in disbelief at me and not moving in any manner as if to attack me. They were in some sort of superstitious shock. The rage or demon that had consumed me did not care if they now were helpless and not wanting to battle. I walked up to the one on my right as he said his death chant in the Ute language that at the time I did not understand, but I could read his eyes and I knew he was preparing himself for death; I slit his throat before he could finish.

The sixth and final warrior dropped to his knees as he now proceeded to prepare himself for the afterlife. Still consumed by the demon rage, I did not kill this warrior and walked over to him and grabbed him by his long hair and brought his head closer to me and I sliced off his right ear. I then pushed him away and with swinging my arms indicated he should stand and leave. In my crazed state of mind, I had now just declared war on the whole Ute Indian nation, and I needed this one to live and tell the tale of what happened here at the mouth of La Caverna Del Oro.

In fear, the last remaining Ute Indian backed away still watching me as I went to all of his fallen friends and proceeded to cut the right ear off of each of the Ute warriors. I wanted to mark them in such a way that they knew that it was me who had killed their brothers, sons, and fathers.

The last warrior finally realized I was letting him go and I can only imagine what thoughts ran through his mind, but once he realized I was only going to take his right ear and not his life, he after several failed attempts, mounted his horse. He quickly put his horse into a trot and left as fast as his horse could carry him.

Battered and bloody I tried to reason and ponder what had just happened in the last day and night. After killing the Indians and for the time being after the battle, I was safe and this knowledge did nothing to please me. I was still angry and the rage was still there. I knew on that day that Matt Lee - the man I was - no longer existed and had become something else, something that I was not proud of.

CHAPTER 8

Stopping my tale once again to drink some water, I could not even form a spit ball my mouth had become so dry. All those present during the telling of my early years seemed mystified and in some sort of shock. All their faces were blank except Walk With Ghost since she already knew the whole story.

After drinking a full glass of water that had been offered by Sherol Roy, I began again, "Losing track of time, but looking back on it, I would say it was two or three days that I stayed at the kill site in front of La Caverna Del Oro. I never once entered the cave again. My mind was lost in a constant rage of hatred, but I had enough wits about me to know that the cave and what dwelled inside would consume what little I had left of what use to be me. I buried my friends Jay, Dan, and Sam in one grave just to the south of the entrance to the cave. Mike I left where he had died in the cave, because I did not have the courage to go back in and get his body. I will always carry that guilt of that with me until my death. The Ute Indians minus their right ears lay where they had died in battle without my giving it a second thought.

The Ute hostiles that Mike and I had killed I would learn in the years following were the best of the best warriors chosen for this one and only role in life and that was to prevent and or kill anyone that located La Caverna Del Oro. Their job was to prevent what roamed within the walls of the isolated cave from being spread among their people.

The Ute warrior that I spared had spread the word of what happened and with the telling and retelling over a short period of time, the legend of "Ghost" was born. They believed that I was not human because "Ghost" had taken two arrows to the chest and had not been killed. Not only had I not been killed, but savagely fought and killed five of their greatest warriors single handedly in one battle. Over the next two years all the original tribes - Parianucs, Yampa, Capote, Weeminuche, Tabeguache, and the Uintahs would become my enemy and "Ghost" would become the Ute Indian nation's greatest enemy. And because "Ghost" was such a daunting foe, they then saw themselves as great warriors to have such a formidable foe to fight.

For the next two years I became "Ghost" and something I am here to tell you tonight I was not proud of. I didn't live in the darkness, but there was a darkness that lived within me. On that day and night on Marble Mountain, I learned what no man should learn and that evil, demons, and ghosts truly live within us all and we battle the good and evil every day within our souls. Sometimes we step off the edge of madness and the evil wins. It was as if my newly declared war on the Ute Indian nation was what I was born to do and for the next couple of years of my life - that life as Ghost – it was as if I was in a dream fog with only one vision of clarity and that was to war with the Utes. In my madness I walked the line between the sane and those not sane; the biggest part of me felt the rage and the chaos and it overshadowed the part that was still sane and was the man Matt Lee."

My mouth had become dry again, and I quickly downed another full glass of water. Looking at the expressions of my friends seated around the table at the Baldwin Hotel, I saw different reactions etched in their faces.

Walk With Ghost, who already knew the story and loved me unconditionally, wore an expression of loving concern for me as she knew how haunted I was of all things that had passed. Chance, a man I knew that was more like me than he would probably like to admit, showed concern for his old friend and mentor. He knew of the evil that goes on inside of men like us, for he had glimpsed it some in his hatred for the Biggers and Hammond gang as he hunted down and killed each and every one of those that had did him and or his wrong. Roger Baldwin, a man I had not met until this day, showed concern also; not knowing his past, I suspected he also had struggled a time or two with that evil that dwells within all of us. The women Sherol Roy and Kellie Shawn Arriaga showed the horror of the events that I spoke of - not hatred for me - but horror of the fate that seemed to have chosen me.

Knowing I could not stop telling my story even if I wanted to, I had for some reason the need to speak of it now, and bear it all in front of those seated here at the table, so I began again, "The Ute Indians were a proud people and felt it was only fitting to send their greatest warriors to battle me one at a time. Never in the next two years would I fight more than one of their warriors at a time. It was their way of honoring me in their warrior creed and culture. As much as they hated me, they also respected my warrior skill.

Within days of leaving the kill site and the haunted La Caverna Del Oro, I was presented with my first challenge of a fight to the death.

I remember him clearly as he sat on his fully painted war pony across a very small stream from me on a late summer afternoon. He truly was an intimidating looking fellow with long black ebony hair tied into one braid with two eagle feathers woven into the end of his braid. His war paint consisted of red and blues that gave this warrior of the Ute nation an eerie face mask. If I had to guess, he probably weighed in about 210 pounds or so and I could see his forearms ripple with muscle in the late day's sun. He was armed with only a tomahawk and knife with no bow, arrows or lance. This, as we both knew as we looked into each other's eyes, was a fight to the death in the old way of hand-to-hand combat.

Dismounting my horse with only my own tomahawk and knife, I made my way to the stream's edge and swung my arms in an intimidating way to loosen up my arms. The chaos and madness that now was within my mind knew that no matter what happened, I would be the victor here in this fight. Feeling immortal or that maybe I had really died in that cave right along with Mike Sands, my mind knew here - right now in this moment of time - that I was unbeatable.

The fierce Ute Indian warrior sat on his horse on the far bank and as capable as he may have been as soon as he dismounted and came within a few yards of me, I could read the fear he felt about me in his eyes. He stank of fear and I smelled that too. He knew that he was going to die at my hands today in the fading light of this late summer day. He knew it and I knew it, but he was a warrior nonetheless and would fight me. It was his destiny and with a war cry that shook the heavens, he started at a full run into the stream to reach me.

Leaving the bank with no such war cry for courage, I also entered into the chilled knee deep mountain water, and we met in the middle. With his tomahawk raised above his head with a killing strike in his right hand and his knife held to deliver an up thrust from below, we collided chest to chest with such force, it seemed to take the air out of the Ute warrior's lungs as he gasped for air and dropped his knife into the flowing water. I easily blocked his blow with the tomahawk with my left hand and arm and thrust upward with my right hand, which held my own knife and entered into his chest and stabbed into his heart. All of the Ute warrior's muscles went soft as he started to bleed out. He was still alive and looking at me as I lowered his now dying body into the water as I cut off his right ear. I saw his life slowly ebb away as his body started to float downstream.

I knew on that day in that small stream just north of Marble Mountain in the Sangre de Cristo Mountains that my war against the Ute Indian nation had begun.

The Ute warriors made it easy for me; I did not have to hunt them because they came willingly to me. To kill me, they would become the greatest warrior the Utes had ever seen. To die at my hand, they were still assured of high stature in their society and a special place in their spirit world.

For the next two years of my life after that fateful encounter at La Caverna Del Oro, I rode my madness across the Rocky Mountain frontier living the life as the feared enemy – Ghost."

CHAPTER 9

M y mouth had once again gone dry and my mind was full of images from my past during my days of insanity. After downing another full glass of water that had been offered by Sherol, I handed her back the glass and as I looked in her eyes, I saw concern and maybe a touch of fear. I smiled at her to reassure her that the madness I felt in those days had long passed from me and that the man known as Matt Lee was now in control.

Walk With Ghost touched my arm lovingly and told me to finish the story. Clearing my voice, I began again, "The two years that followed seem almost like a dream now. I never went back to trap for William Bent and Ceran St. Vrain, for I was sure they would not even recognize me in the state I was in.

I lived off the land and never during that time did I reach out and try to establish any type of contact with any man or woman. During this time of insanity and revenge, I never spoke one word to anyone. I did not speak English for a full two years. The only contact I had was when one of the Utes' mightiest warriors would hunt me down to defend the pride of the Ute people. And in each and every encounter, I was the victor and they would die by my hand.

Only using my Hawkins rifle to kill game for food, I never used it in my fights with the Ute warriors. These savage fights to death were all hand-to-hand in the most brutal and murderous way. My days were filled with rage and hatred, and those days quickly became months, and before I knew it two years had passed.

After each of their warrior's death, I would always mark those by cutting off their right ears so my enemy knew "Ghost" had killed their very best in battle. I kept the ears in a leather pouch and would count them every night for two years…13, 14, 15, all the way to 21 ears. I was not sickened by the sight of the ears nor did they make me happy. I just counted them. The rage and hatred made me count them and in a way it seemed like payment to me as if I had earned them somehow.

Deep inside of me, I knew the killing, rage, hatred, and the cutting off of the ears was not normal and was immoral, and I tried to reach that part of me that believed in the Lord above and find the goodness of my childhood bible teachings.

Years later I would understand that we all have this good dog and evil dog that reside in us and the one that wins is the one you feed the most. During my time of rage, the evil dog was never hungry.

Wandering the Rocky Mountains, I was lost, not in the sense of physical direction; that I had no difficulty with. Instead, I was lost in the sense of having only one purpose in life and that was to be the enemy of the Ute Indians that had killed my friends on Marble Mountain."

At this point I reached over and adoringly touched Walk With Ghost, the woman that saved me from myself. No one here, even after hearing my story, would ever understand my love for this woman. Walk With Ghost gave me her light and she forgave my darkness.

After sipping some more water, I continued my story, "In those years of madness, I had drifted north, never leaving the Rockies since they were now my home, but north I drifted. The

Ute Indian nation was vast with all the original tribal bands claiming almost if not all of the Rocky Mountain frontier and by drifting north, I crossed over into what we now call the Grand River Utes' ancestral land. Where we sit tonight here in Grand Lake was part of their land; it stretched from as far south as Rollins Pass to just north of the Kawuneeche Valley and east to west from the "Great Divide" to just short of Hot Sulphur Springs.

In my second summer after the ordeal in the haunted cave at Marble Mountain, I had crossed over the "Great Divide" going east to west over Rollins Pass into the Middle Park basin area. Making camp on the floor of the valley and as was my custom when reaching a new area, I had set some snares for small game such as rabbits and such.

Just an hour after dawn on a late summer day, I was walking the high bank of a small pond checking my snares and as I walked to the edge of the bank and down below me just on the other side of the pond, I saw an Indian. Suddenly my rage topped out again as I crouched in the high summer grass to watch my new foe and to plan my attack.

The Indian dismounted and I soon realized this was no warrior sent to kill the "Ghost." Studying the smaller Indian, I realized before long that I was looking at a woman wearing a buckskin dress with lots of fringe for decoration. She was a very beautiful woman and she was young like me; her hair was coal black with two braids that reached to the middle of her back. She was a small and petite woman and by her movement when she walked, I could tell she was powerful and very agile and not frail for someone so little. She turned towards me but could not see the "Ghost" hiding in the tall summer grass, but I could see her fully and she was so lovely it mesmerized me. Even from the distance I saw the color of her eyes and they were the color of the acorns that fall from the trees.

Watching this Indian woman, my future wife - then known as "Little Crow" - brought happiness to a heart that had forgotten what happiness was.

Little Crow let her horse graze the summer grass around the pond at will, and she took off her moccasins and lifted her dress enough to walk in the water calf high. I watched her with all her beauty and innocence; just being there brought tears to my eyes. It

44

was as if the blanket of rage had been lifted off of me and I was filled with something I had not felt in a long time - joy.

After cooling her feet in the chilled water, Little Crow sat down on the bank and still facing me as I hid in the tall grass, she turned her perfect face toward the sun and closed her eyes soaking up the sun's rays. Keeping this image of her perfection etched in my mind, I closed my eyes and did the same. More tears came as I remembered how during my rage and chaos of the last couple of years, I had forgotten the simple pleasures of life - like the warmth of the sun on my face.

Opening my eyes, I was somewhat afraid that it had been just a vision and she really was not there, but a smile crossed my face as I realized she did in fact exist. She was still there sunning herself. I hoped her horse would not sense me and alert her to my presence so she would flee. I was very much content in watching her from afar. The last thing I wanted was to frighten her.

My tears, more than I would like to admit, flowed while watching her and I could feel her goodness, and I was convinced she was heaven sent to give me this vision to subdue the evil dog that had control of me. Somehow, someway this vision, this angel helped me remember my faith in all the good things in life and in the heavens. On this day and at that moment was a surprise when the good dog in me came forth to be fed. I welcomed this surprise since I had become weary with death and rage and of feeding the malevolent dog. This Indian woman, whom I did not know, had changed me and opened my heart once again. I pondered deeply on how that could be?

Leaning back onto her elbows still taking in the sun's warmth on her face, Little Crow stretched out her legs into the water and lightly splashed the water with her feet. She seemed so at peace without a care and one with nature at this moment that all I could do was stare at her in this moment of bliss.

Watching her, I felt at peace as if I was sitting on that bank with her with my feet in the water. Out of the corner of my eye, I saw her mare jerk her head up from grazing with her ears standing straight up and at full attention. Did her mare sense me? I wondered?

Her mare was not looking at me, but behind Little Crow at the tree line, I followed her gaze and at first I did not see what the danger was. Then I saw movement just inside the timberline - tan colored fur with slender strong muscular limbs. It did not take me long to realize a mountain lion was now stalking the Indian woman.

CHAPTER 10

S tanding and waving my arms to warn the Indian girl or distract the mountain lion or both failed because even though Little Crow was facing me, she still had her eyes closed and the mountain lion in his crouched position was concentrated on his next kill. I tried to yell, but after two years of not speaking, it came out badly and was a low whimper. I am sure I looked and sounded like some mad man, which now looking back was only fitting.

In a panic for the woman I would get to know as Little Crow, I started to sprint taking out my tomahawk and knife. Little Crow finally noticed me, but not the mountain lion as I leaped from the tall bank to the edge of the pond and in an all-out sprint, I raced around the pond in her direction.

Little Crow was still leaning back on her elbows and was slow to move as she was startled, then fearful as I advanced on her in my sprint. During my race to face the lion, I tried to put Little

Crow to the back of my mind and ready myself for battle with the lion. Several things zig zagged through my mind when battling wild critters. When bears attack, it's usually a territorial thing, but when mountain lions attack, they mean to kill you. Playing dead most often satisfies a grizzly bear, which then wanders off to its regular business. Playing dead for a mountain lion just lets them finish the job. I knew fighting a mountain lion was a battle to the death, something I was well versed in.

The mountain lion was so focused on Little Crow that it had not sensed me yet and when I was still several yards away, the mountain lion sprang its attack on Little Crow sinking its razor sharp teeth into the top of her left shoulder and once having a firm grip started to shake her back and forth trying to tear off a chunk of meat. I saw Little Crow's eyes roll-up and go blank as she passed out.

Even though my voice had long been rusty, I was able to summon up a fearsome battle cry as I closed the distance on the mountain lion. Hearing me and seeing me for the first time, the lion let loose of Little Crow and turned to face this new threat.

Still sprinting and never slowing down, I ran headlong into the mountain lion as it reared up to meet me, and I was chest to chest before it had a chance to swipe at me with those dagger-like claws. My forward progress was so powerful when colliding with the mountain lion, I dropped my tomahawk from my left hand. My knife was in my right hand and with an underhand grip, I stabbed with all the muscle the Lord gave me into the left side of the lion just behind the shoulder where I believed the heart to be. My left forearm had ended up in the mountain lion's mouth and with all my strength I pushed its head back not letting it get a good grip and bite down. Not feeling the pain yet, I knew the sharp teeth had made several punctures into my arm. Not pulling out my knife, I just stirred it some while inserted into the flesh until I nicked the heart of the beast. Once the heart was punctured, the mountain lion's muscles went slack as it started to bleed out inside. Still keeping the pressure on with my left forearm forcing its head back to keep the mountain lion from biting down, I waited the few seconds until the lion's eyes went blank as its life faded and finally extinguished before pulling out my knife.

I lowered the lion's body to the ground slowly so I did not end up with more puncture wounds in my left forearm than I already had. Once I had freed my forearm and after quickly studying my injuries and deciding that although severe, none of the main rivers that pumped blood had been punctured. I then turned my attention to the young Indian girl."

Walk With Ghost's eyes filled with tears as she remembered the day and the attack from the mountain lion. Sherol Roy and Kellie Shawn were quick to comfort her. Looking at Walk With Ghost and remembering her as that young girl Little Crow drained me since I was once again feeling the peaks and valleys of the emotions of that day so many years ago. Sherol took the time in the break of my telling the tale to gather up some roasted turkey for us to eat.

Stepping out onto the front porch to smoke some tobacco in my corn cob pipe with Chance, I realized that dawn was fast approaching. I was lost in thought when Chance spoke, "I had no idea Matt Lee. Why did you never mention any of this before? Does Lucas know all about this? Yours and Walk With Ghost's story?"

After pulling hard on the pipe to get a lung full, I had to wait a moment before I could speak. Looking at Chance, "Yes, Lucas knows and has met Walk With Ghost and as the good friend that he is, he respected my wishes to never talk about those days. The only good that came from those dark days was my love for that woman in there. I feel no pride in all the other; I feel ashamed of the madness. Walk With Ghost is the only thing that keeps me sane."

Chance slowly nodded his head "yes" as if he understood. Not sure if he did; hell, I am not sure even if I did. Turning I walked back in and found my seat at the table again. After drinking a full glass of water and clearing my voice, "Little Crow was still out, but breathing and after looking at her wound to the top of her shoulder, I realized how bad it really was. She was bleeding gravely, and I knew she needed some serious care, knowing she would die before any of her people could find her. Her only chance at living was me. Using my knife, I cut the bottom of her dress off to use as a bandage and dressed her wound as best as I could until I could get her back to my campsite.

Her pinto mare was spooked from my sudden appearance and the ensuing battle with the mountain lion and of course the smell of blood. It took more time than I wanted to be able to finally coax the mare in close enough to calm the horse down. The mare started to spook again as I loaded the wounded Little Crow on her back, but I kept reassuring the horse with my newly found soothing voice and gentle touches to her neck and mane. Once safely loaded, I moved Little Crow to my campsite less than a mile to the north.

Once I got back to my campsite with Little Crow, I started a fire, not because it was cold, but because I would need the red hot blade of my knife to stop her bleeding. My next task was to make her as comfortable as possible while the fire made the coals needed to heat the blade. After making a comfortable bed of evergreen boughs, I gently lowered her down and that is when her eyes sprung open. Little Crow was startled to see me this close, but did not try and fight me. It only took her a second or two to realize I probably had saved her life and was doing the best to help doctor her. I tried to speak to her, but it was evident she spoke no English and of course I did not speak Ute.

Fear was in her eyes - not from me - but from her realizing her wound was life threatening. Once the blade of my knife was red hot, I showed it to her and she nodded "yes" knowing what I had to do. I used my left hand to pin her down as I applied the knife not once, but three times to stop the bleeding wounds over the course of several minutes as I had to reheat the knife each time. She cried the first time and kicked out with all her might and promptly passed out from the pain.

For the next couple of weeks, I seemed to have lost all my rage and felt no need to hate the Ute Indians anymore. My sole purpose during that time was taking care of Little Crow and getting her back healthy. It felt good to care again about something and someone. Knowing I had walked the trail of madness, I pretended not to care for Little Crow as much as I did. I knew full well there would come the time she was healthy enough to rejoin her people and it scared me, because I was not sure how to handle that.

We both used this time to teach each other our language. Through a lot of pointing and just downright guessing, I started to learn Ute and she started to learn English.

Being as young as I was and with no experience with women in general and during those years of madness, I had lost all want in a woman. Didn't think I needed one. After feeling like I was a dead man walking, Little Crow in a few short weeks made me feel alive again.

I did not want to admit it; I hated to admit it. Never had experience with it, but I realized something…I was falling in love with Little Crow and it scared the hell out of me!"

CHAPTER 11

R eturning to the present for a moment and looking at Walk With Ghost, I could still see the love in her eyes for me even after 30 plus years. I knew in my heart the reason we had remained together all these years is that we both got something from being a couple. On my part I needed her; she made me sane. My wife was still as beautiful and innocent as the first time I saw her on the day of the mountain lion attack and again pondered what she got out of being with me and once again I drew a blank. It was something, but I had always been afraid to ask her. Wiping the one tear from her eye as she smiled at me, I turned back to the others seated at the table and cleared my throat again, "As you can surmise Little Crow survived the ordeal with the mountain lion."

That brought smiles from the group and Chance rolled his right hand and fingers in a "get on with it" motion as he spoke, "No Shit Matt Lee - you're killing us here. Then, what happened?"

Feeling more comfortable in the telling after speaking of the dark years was done, I began again, "Like I said it had been the end of the summer of that fateful day of the mountain lion attack, but in the high mountain air as we all know wounds heal faster and are not prone to infection as much so Little Crow healed fast.

She was more than healthy enough to rejoin her people within about ten days. During that time we became accustomed to each other and learned more than enough of both of our languages that we communicated very well. Even though we both knew she was well enough to leave, she didn't. She did not want to leave and I wanted her to stay.

I never hid the fact of who I was as the nemesis of her people, and Little Crow knew that it was "Ghost," the sworn enemy of all the Ute tribes, who also was the one who had fought and killed a mountain lion to save her. I never understood how she could look past my hatred and rage and still find the goodness of my heart, but she did. I will never be able to explain it, other than it was meant to be, that something greater than Little Crow and myself was in play. Over the years and spending countless hours pondering on it, the answer always escaped me and in time I just quit thinking about it.

During the time of her healing and it is even still true today, we rarely spoke of my past. Never really wanted to touch on what led up to my dark days. I have always felt the madness and the darkness will always be there just beyond my touch, but still too close for comfort. Without Walk With Ghost here, I would have never even attempted to speak of those dark times tonight.

During this time together I learned a great deal of my future wife. She was a princess of the Grand River Utes since her father was the Chief. She had two siblings - one sister Falling Rain and one brother Piah, who as we all know now is the Chief of the so called renegade Utes.

We were in hiding at the time; neither of us wanted to be found by her people. I was afraid what I might do if we were found, and she had the same fear as I. Time quickly passed and the ten days turned into the autumn months and then into the winter months.

In the first two months of being together, I never touched her in a physical way. I wanted her very much so, but I did not want to destroy what we already had. I was fearful of my love for her and never spoke of it, but it was not long before I realized falling in love with her was like the rain; you can see all the signs long before you feel the physical touch of a raindrop as it lands on your upturned face. Fate had put us together that day of the mountain lion attack. It was also fate and destiny that made us fall in love with each other.

Little Crow had changed me without even trying to change me. Her presence in my life brought the good dog in me forward to be fed. I knew full well the hatred and rage had left that day on the banks of that small pond when I watched a young girl joyously walk in the water and enjoy the sun.

That whole winter following the mountain lion attack, we lived as husband and wife and we were very happy. As much as we pretended that it did not exist - it still was there - I was the enemy of her people. It was something that I could not take back. I was "Ghost."

Toward the end of winter with spring fast approaching, I become sullen as Little Crow and I discussed what lay ahead for us in our future. It would not be long before the Utes once again, since the snow started to melt, would send their mightiest and bravest warriors to kill me. Her family and tribe most likely believed that she was dead. We talked about leaving the Rocky Mountains and the land of the Ute, but quickly dismissed that idea because we knew nothing else and had no idea where to go.

There was a nagging feeling pulling on me that if I left the area, I would never be free from what I had done. I no longer had the leather pouch of ears from the warriors that I had slain in battle; those had been buried with a prayer long ago in the first week after Little Crow became part of my life.

We decided no; well, that's not true, I decided and Little Crow against her better judgement went along with it. It was decided that for us to find any happiness at all that I had to ask for forgiveness from those that wanted me dead. As crazy as it sounds, I would lay down my weapons and offer myself to my enemy. If I died at their hands, so be it. To die for the sins I had committed against their people would not wash away the shame and guilt that I felt, but it would be a fitting death for what I now saw as crimes against the Ute Indian nation.

Believe me my friends, at that moment of making the decision that more likely than not would bring my death, I felt fear. Before saving Little Crow and with my mind in chaos and rage, I felt immortal and invincible. When the rage and chaos left, I sensed and felt mortal again. Somehow she had brought back my humanity and I became Matt Lee again, and that crazed fellow that was "Ghost" was pushed far back just out of reach. It was as if the demon from La Caverna Del Oro or just the evil dog that resided in me had gone back to where it came from. I now had control again. If death was what awaited me then I welcomed it - feared it - but welcomed it.

The day we left our winter camp I actually felt joy, for I knew whatever fate and destiny had in store for me, that the madness was now gone. Either way the rage, chaos, or the insanity would be never more.

That day of leaving our camp more than thirty years ago still feels just like yesterday to me. The sun had broken through the clouds that morning, and I could feel the warmth on my face as I looked toward the heavens. The forever blue sky grew larger as the clouds drifted to places unknown. I could hear the water dripping almost silently from the evergreen boughs as the warm sun melted the last remaining snow of the season. The air, although with a slight chill, smelled like life renewing itself with a new day of spring. It was a glorious day to be alive.

By mid-afternoon we had located the winter camp of Little Crow's people, the Grand River Utes on the floor of the Middle Park Basin. We could smell and see the smoke of the camp and cook fires. Stopping about 50 yards to the east of the camp, I studied the camp, which held more than 60 teepees, and their war horses in the makeshift corral were more than I could count.

Mounted on our horses in the open white winter landscape with the nearest tree line more than 100 yards away, we were easily spotted.

Loud voices and shouts could be heard coming from the winter camp and within a few minutes, six warriors mounted on painted war ponies cautiously approached us.

When the Ute warriors got within twenty yards, I could hear Little Crow as she was choked with emotion. The warrior leading the six was her brother Piah and he wore the breast plate of the chieftain, which meant her father had died in her absence. Little Crow raised both of her hands in a stop motion and Chief Piah and the rest came to a sudden stop. I could see in their eyes they were confused as hell. First, it had to be a shock to see Little Crow still alive after having disappeared many months prior, but more so that she was with their greatest enemy "Ghost." From their faces, there was no doubt they knew who I was.

Slowly and with care I dismounted my mare and locked eyes with Chief Piah and showing no fear walked closer to his war pony. The mare of Little Crow's brother and now chief of the Grand River Utes started to fidget and throw her head as I approached. After Chief Piah was able to calm his mare, he drew his tomahawk in his right hand.

When I was about five yards away, I showed him my Hawkins 50 caliber rifle outstretched with both hands and slowly laid it on the ground. Having done that, I slowly drew both my tomahawk and knife and tossed them both to the ground right next to my Hawkins rifle.

Still with our eyes locked on one another, I lowered myself to my knees in front of him and closed my eyes and I bowed before him."

CHAPTER 12

I was sure that Chief Piah and the five warriors with him must have thought me mad at that moment, but as I bowed before him silently saying the Lord's Prayer in my mind, I knew it was the sanest thing that I had ever done.

In asking for forgiveness from my enemies, I had found once again my faith. No matter what would happen in the following few minutes - be it life or death - I was okay with the outcome. I knew the Lord was my savior at this very moment and if it was his will to call me home I would accept it with an open heart.

With my eyes still closed, I could hear the horses shuffling their feet and snorting as Chief Piah and the others tried to figure out what to do with such an unusual circumstance.

Finally I could hear Chief Piah dismount his mare and the undeniable sound of drawing his knife from a leather scabbard on his right side, so now he would have a choice of using either the tomahawk or knife to end my life. So it would seem death was what awaited me, and my only regret was that Little Crow would have to watch me die.

I could feel the tip of Chief Piah's tomahawk at the base of my skull where it meets the top of my shoulders as if he was measuring his arm swing to deal a killing blow. I was not scared, for in accepting my fate, I had set all fear of dying aside.

Knowing what I had become the last two years sickened me at this moment of my impending death and somehow I felt this was how it was supposed to be.

With his tip of his tomahawk still resting at the base of my skull, Chief Piah spoke in his native tongue, but not to me. He spoke in a voice with concern to his sister Little Crow, "Little Crow are you a ghost too?"

Little Crow responded in a calm voice, "No my brother, I am alive as you are. The enemy of our people saved me from an attacking mountain lion and "Ghost" fought it with his bare hands and a knife. He saved my life and brought me back from the edge of death."

Chief Piah, still talking to his sister as I bowed before him with my head at the end of his tomahawk, "He offers himself to me in this way and I think he knows he cannot be killed. He is "Ghost." He is still the enemy of our people."

In a more forceful tone, "Not true my brother. He offers you his life and asks forgiveness. He is not a ghost. He is a man just like you. He bleeds red just like you."

The silence for the next minute weighed heavily in the air as Chief Piah must have been pondering what Little Crow had said. I felt pressure as Little Crow's brother pushed down, then suddenly with a quick jerk of his tomahawk, he cut me. I could feel the warmth of my blood as it trickled down the side of my face.

With his tomahawk Chief Piah stuck it under my chin and forced me backwards from a bowing position to my knees. With blood still flowing from the wound on the back of my neck, I opened my eyes to face Chief Piah.

Chief Piah, though young and about my age, had the bearing of all great men. Standing before me was a man that could have been a general of a Roman legion or a commander of the French army. His mere presence commanded respect and honor. His hair was long and black and was braided into two braids with four eagle feathers woven into the braids on each side. He wore doe skin pants and a long sleeve doe skin shirt fringed with colorful beads and small eagle bones. His elaborate breast plate foretold of his importance as Chief among the Grand River Ute Indians. The breastplate was made of eagle bones for a warrior's wisdom and clarity, with a few grizzly claws thrown in for strength and power. He seemed strong and in command of all that was around him and I could see the intelligence of the man flicker in his eyes. I had no doubt that Chief Piah could be a deadly adversary if the need should arise. I was proud to offer my life to such a warrior.

With his tomahawk still under my chin, Chief Piah said with curiosity in his voice, "You are not a ghost? You are a man?"

Surprising myself and with a very calm voice I replied, "I am a man just like you. I have come here today to offer you my life and ask forgiveness of you for any grief and suffering I may have caused the women and children of the Ute for taking the lives of their husbands and fathers as they died a glorious death in battle. After the battle and death of my friends at La Caverna Del Oro, I felt rage and hate that I was not use to, and it took your sister Little Crow to rid me of the demon that resided in my soul. She says I saved her, but I am here to tell you, she saved me. My life is yours if you want it."

Chief Piah squinted his eyes and he put some pressure backwards on his tomahawk as he spoke, "Tell me Ghost, if you are not a ghost or a demon, but a man, why should I not kill you?"

Knowing I had no good answer for the Chief of the Grand River Utes, "I offer you nothing that you do not already have. You have the knowledge of the chiefs that have gone before you and the love of your people. You are a mighty warrior for all of those that know you. Nothing I say today will change any of that. I can make you a promise and that is I will hunt and fight for you. You already know my greatness as a warrior. The thing that weighs heavily on my mind is that I will serve and protect your sister until the last breath that I breathe. I swear to my Lord and your Great Spirit that to be true."

Still on my knees in front of Chief Piah, I spread out my arms as if I was on a crucifix, "I respect you Chief Piah, but I tire of this talk and if it is my life you want, take it now."

Chief Piah squinted his eyes as if in deep thought and still undecided on my fate asked in a calm voice, "You speak our tongue. How is this possible?"

With my arms still stretched out and looking Piah in the eyes, "Your sister not only saved me from what I was, but she also taught me your tongue and much of your way of life."

Shaking his head in a slow "yes" motion, Chief Piah put his tomahawk and knife back in their leather scabbards and motioned me to stand. With our eyes still locked, the Chief of the Grand River Utes was still searching for answers about what lay beneath the exterior of "Ghost," the greatest enemy the Ute people ever had.

Reaching out and grabbing my right shoulder, he surprised me as he started to speak in perfect English, "If what I heard today is true and you saved my sister from a certain death, then I shall spare your life. You have shown me more courage and strength today than any man I have known offering your life for me to take. I have much to learn of the white man's ways. I fear they are a flood upon the land of the Ute that cannot be stopped. You will teach me how they think and why they act the way they do."

Looking at everyone that was seated here now in the this early Rocky Mountain morning in Grand Lake at the Baldwin Hotel, I knew they had heard the story of "Ghost" and probably one of the strangest tales of a man's life that they had ever heard before. Now in the telling of my story and having just relived all the memories in my mind, I felt relief in telling others of the twist and turns my life had taken. Kellie Shawn was the first that spoke, "In all the years together with Little Crow...I mean Walk With Ghost, did you ever have children?"

Walk With Ghost laid her head on my shoulder and looked directly at Kellie Shawn and spoke quietly as if it hurt to speak, "Two beautiful sons, that were handsome and smart and were boys to be proud of, but not very good warriors. Both were killed many years ago fighting the Arapahoes."

Looking down into Walk With Ghost's eyes, "I believed their deaths were somehow a punishment for my years of madness and warfare against the Ute."

It had grown quiet for several minutes as no one really had the words anymore, so Sherol Roy stood with a tear rolling down her cheek and spoke with some emotion with her voice cracking, "It's late or rather it is early. The dawn is not far away and we all need to get some sleep. I have to say that having people in Roger's and my house that we care deeply for has been a welcome relief. Matt Lee, whatever you were before meeting your lovely wife, you are now something to be proud of."

Having said all that she was going to say on the matter, Sherol Roy with a raised arm and motioning with her hand, scooted us all off to our rooms.

CHAPTER 13

After breakfast sitting on the front porch of the Baldwin Hotel and smoking my corn cob pipe with Chance, Roger, and the half wolf Mutt, I could see the comings and goings of the whole settlement of Grand Lake this early spring morning.

We all had slept late due to my telling of my past life, and the sun was already at the mid-morning point in the sky. Not a cloud in the sky and very little wind to carry the "tree whispers," but the undeniable chirp, chirp sounds of some close Mountain Chickadees could be heard reminding me how life was renewed in the spring each season. The tiny birds with black caps, white cheeks, and black throats were entertaining to watch as they hung upside down to get at the undersides of branches, cones, and needles. Spring in the Rockies was a good season to walk the mountains and be alive. Laughing to myself, I thought, "Hell, any season, above ground is good."

Sitting down on one of the pine wood benches to refill my pipe, I heard Roger Baldwin ask, "What's next for you fellows? Where are you headed from here?"

Chance spoke first, "Kellie Shawn and I will head out today to Hot Sulphur Springs to finish buying the land to start building her brother's ranch. Kellie had not completed the deal before her body guards and friends were killed by the last remaining members of the Biggers and Hammond gang. Hopefully the land is still available; I am sure the owners thought the whole deal had gone sour after Kellie Shawn had been kidnapped by the outlaw Rick Alvardo. If the land has been sold, then the mission would be to find a different place to start to build."

A smile broke out on Roger's face, "That is wonderful Chance, and if you both stay in the Middle Park Basin area, we will be neighbors and hopefully get to see you, Kellie Shawn, and Mutt from time to time."

Roger now turned his gaze and attention my way, "And you Matt Lee, what does the future hold for yourself and Walk With Ghost?"

I looked at Roger and Chance as I pondered if they would understand what Walk With Ghost and I were planning on doing and if they would think it a waste of time. I guess in the end, I really did not care what anyone thought, only what I thought to be the best for Walk With Ghost and myself. Speaking with an even voice, "With more and more white people getting upset with the Ute Indians and their refusal to go to the reservation, my main goal is to protect Walk With Ghost, just like I promised her brother Chief Piah over 30 years ago. Nothing of that promise has ever changed. Our sons are long dead, and the only thing Walk With Ghost and I have in this world is each other. We realize we are not young anymore and our plan is simple; we just want to live our lives out in some sort of peaceful harmony. Many years ago I found a hidden valley on the eastern side of Boreas Pass, up above the town of Como, but just below timberline. I believe Walk With Ghost and I are the only humans that have ever walked in the valley. It has high walls and protection from the wind and plenty of fresh water from springs that flow from the mountain itself. Wild game a plenty for two people without ever leaving the valley. Walk With Ghost and I have never been about worldly possessions, only about what nature can provide. Years ago I started a cabin there. We plan on finishing it and living there far from those that hate the Indians. We have even given the valley the name Redemption for the obvious reasons. I realize it will not be long before the culture of the Ute Indian is long dead, but the hatred for the Indian will always remain. When it is our time, we will die and become dust in our valley, our little slice of heaven. I don't think it is too much to ask."

Roger and Chance both took in what I had just said and nodded their heads in a "yes" motion as if they understood. Everything I have done in my life since I watched a young Indian girl soak in the sun and walk in the cool water of that distant pond has been to honor and protect the woman that saved me from myself. I owed her my life and I would happily take a bullet to save hers. Whatever I did in that regard would never be enough, but it was my will to try. I loved her like no other and always have...always will.

Standing to tap my corn cob pipe on the top railing of the porch to loosen the burnt tobacco to clean it and looking toward the west, I saw four troopers from the Colorado 3rd enter the town. As they rode their mounts past the Baldwin Hotel, I figured each and every trooper could not have been older than 18 - young, dumb, heavily armed, and on the prod for renegade Ute Indians. Counting the five U.S. Cavalry mounts I saw in town yesterday when we entered and the number that just passed the hotel, I figured there were a total of nine troopers in Grand Lake. Counting the full troop of 95 we saw just as we were leaving the Kawuneeche Valley, it looked as if the Cavalry was building a presence and a force to be reckoned with here to deal with renegade Utes and my brother-in-law Chief Piah.

No need to warn my brother-in-law; he has had Ute scouts out for some time now and would know of all movement in the Middle Park Basin and Kawuneeche Valley. My hope would be that he would head to the reservation in Utah, because if he chose to fight there would be plenty of young troopers just like the ones that just rode by killed in the name of glory. Of course, the renegades were outnumbered and may not survive any type of sustained war campaign against them. As more troops flooded into the area, the more chance of a fight. And more reason to take Walk With Ghost to our valley at Boreas Pass and away from those that thought the only good Indian was a dead Indian.

As I was thinking about what all the troopers in the area meant in terms of the Ute renegades and in a roundabout way my wife, I watched a man ride up to the Baldwin Hotel. He tied off his horse to the hitching post and made his way up the steps. Chance and Roger knew the man and seemed genuinely happy to see him.

Chance was still shaking his hand when he said to me, "Matt Lee I would like you to meet someone. This is Territorial Marshal Eric Robert."

I knew the name because his reputation was well known across the Rocky Mountain frontier, but had never met the man. Eric Robert was well known as a fair and honest lawman who was tougher than nails and very dangerous with his Colt 44 pistol that was tied down to his right leg with the grip pointed backwards for a standard draw, and the metal shined like the owner knew how to take care of his weapons. As I shook his hand, I could feel his steel like grip. Marshal Robert was about my age and looked like he was about 6'2" and weighed about 190 pounds. He walked with the agility and grace that you might find in a dancer. His hair was short and gray and he had a week's worth of an almost pure white beard. On his mare he was armed heavily with two rifle scabbards, one hosting a lever action Winchester like mine and the other with what looked like a double barrel 12-gauge Greener shotgun. It was obvious by his demeanor and his choice of weapons he was not a man to be trifled with. Still shaking his hand, I said, "I know you by reputation Marshal Robert and that you are a fair and honest lawman."

Eric Robert studied me as I studied him measuring the man behind the reputation. "Matt Lee! One of the most famous men in the Rockies. It is my pleasure to finally get to know the famous man the Ute Indians call "Ghost." Guess I never have heard why they call you that."

Not wanting to relive the story again I replied, "Maybe a story for another time and place Marshal."

Roger broke the slight tension that was building between Marshal Robert and myself when two men like us were sizing the other up by asking, "You need a room Marshal? We do have a vacancy if needed."

Breaking eye contact with me, Marshal Robert turned towards Roger and said, "I do Mr. Baldwin for a week or two. Our office in Denver is worried about the Colorado 3rd troop buildup in Grand Lake as they try to find a solution to Chief Piah and his renegades. As you know the soldiers have a way of getting themselves into trouble when away from home and barracks. I am supposed to keep the peace here in Grand Lake if I can."

CHAPTER 14

I
t was not long before Kellie Shawn Arriaga and Chance Bondurant were ready to leave for their destination of Hot Sulphur Springs. Since it was only a couple of days' ride, they would not need any more supplies.

The women - Kellie Shawn, Walk With Ghost, and Sherol Roy - had a tougher time with the emotions of leaving than the men, but we all knew in this day and age, with distances being long and the difficulty of rough terrain and weather in the Rocky Mountain frontier, this may be the last time any of us saw each other. With kisses and hugs all around and with more than a few good ole' boy back-slaps, Kellie Shawn, Chance and Mutt the half wolf made their way southwest on this fine spring morning.

Walk with Ghost and I left the Baldwin Hotel, but we knew it would be later in the day before we could leave Grand Lake because we would be camping along the trail to our forever home, which we had started to call Redemption Valley, so we needed more supplies and Spirit and Sky needed to be shod. Our destination would cover more miles and was more difficult than Kellie Shawn's and Chance's trail because we had to cross the Great Divide.

In the Morgan Patton Dry Goods store, we were able to purchase the much needed supplies. While we loaded our supplies into saddle bags on the street, none of the soldiers were to be seen and none of the local folks paid much attention to us and that was the way I liked it.

Riding west toward the livery stable, Walk With Ghost and I rode past the Lake Saloon, and we spotted all nine of the U.S. Cavalry mounts that were tied off at the hitching rail in front. The soldier boys were at it early today since it was not even mid-morning yet. Rotgut whiskey, warm beer, and young troopers were never a good mix and I did not envy Marshal Robert's job in trying to keep the peace in Grand Lake.

After we reached the livery stable and settled on a price for Spirit and Sky to get new horse shoes, Howard Smith the owner and I stripped off the saddle bags as Mr. Smith started to size the horses for shoes. Walk With Ghost and I started brushing them down with a wooden curry comb and started to give both the horses a good rub down. Even though they still had their winter coats, I could not help but think how a man and a woman could have asked for any more beautiful horses than these two.

My mare Spirit use to be a Ute Indian war pony. I had won her in an arm wrestling match with my brother in-law Chief Piah. She was a big horse, almost 18 hands tall, chestnut in color except for her right front leg, which had a pure white sock that stretched all the way to her knee. Spirit was fearless, stubborn, and headstrong and liked to have her own way. I put up with her cranky ways because she happened to be the most intelligent horse I had ever seen, bar none. I had owned her for three years now, and we had become accustomed to each other's faults and frankly, I loved her more than any other horse I ever had the pleasure to strap a saddle on.

Walk With Ghost's pinto Sky was a smaller horse that was 15 hands tall, which suited her petite frame nicely. Sky's coloring consisted of three very distinct colors - black, tan, and the typical white splashes that looked as if some crazed person had thrown several buckets of paint on her. Unlike Spirit, Sky was obedient and people-friendly. Sky was probably second only to Spirit as for intelligence in horses that I have owned, which would imply she was smarter than 90 percent of all humans I have ever known.

As Howard was finishing up shoeing the horses, I looked toward the south and watched the thin and wispy clouds as they moved to the west. The sun was now at the midway point and I could feel the warmth tingle my face. The wind was just enough to create some movement of the evergreen boughs, which helped scent the air with the spring like smell of pine.

I watched Walk With Ghost as she coaxed in a couple of wild blue grouse with some fresh wild blueberries she had found at the edge of the lodge pole corral which extended to the edge of the forest. I had never seen a woman or anyone for that matter, who had such a way with wild critters as she did. Other than the day of the mountain lion attack, I have never seen one she could not use her almost magical lure upon. It was almost as if they could sense the goodness in her heart.

The blue grouse were large birds and to my knowledge flew very little, and if they did it was just in short flights to escape prey. I was guessing the two to three pound birds were one male and one female, both with blue-gray mottled brown in color. Both also had a pale gray band on their fan-shaped tail. White markings were present on the flanks and under the tail feathers. Their feathering extended to the base of the middle toe.

After feeding what blueberries she had to the grouse, she stood up and said, "That reminds me Matt Lee, we need some sugar for Spirit and Sky for treats." With that, she took off at a brisk walk east back towards the Morgan Patton Dry Good Store before I could say anything.

Watching as she strolled away, I was once again struck by the fact of how lucky I had become when Walk With Ghost entered my life and how she changed what was to be to what it could be. I pondered about our relationship more than I probably should have. It seemed that everything that I had done in my life and that all my choices and my regrets had led me to that lonely mountain pond that day so I could rescue that young Indian girl. It almost makes my war against the Utes and the madness that overtook me the two years prior to the lion attack almost worth it. If I had done anything, anything at all differently, I might not have met her. My mind was set on finishing our last and remaining years together in our hidden valley - Redemption Valley - far from those that hate the Indians just because they are misunderstood.

Watching Walk With Ghost until she passed by the Lake Saloon where the U.S. Cavalry mounts were and until she walked into the Morgan Patton Dry Goods store and feeling she was safe enough, I turned my attention back to Howard Smith and the horses.

Howard Smith in his deep gravelly voice, "All done Matt Lee and that will be eight bits for the shoeing and six bits for the grain and feed for one day, fourteen bits altogether."

After I paid Mr. Smith, he helped me saddle both Spirit and Sky, and after cinching down the saddle bags with what supplies we had, we spoke some about the weather and the trail south.

Smith asked me where we were headed to the south, and I replied, "Redemption Valley" which brought a very confused look to his face. After twirling that around in his mind for a few seconds, "I have been all around the Colorado Territory in my 64 years and never heard of any place called "Redemption Valley." Are you heading any further south like maybe down into old Mexico?"

Chuckling somewhat to myself, I replied, "No Mr. Smith not as far as Mexico, but far enough south to be far from people."

Mr. Smith, far from being a dumb man, realized that was all he was going to get out of me on that subject and took it at face value and stopped any more inquiry about Walk With Ghost's and my destination. Howard's eyes widened as he suddenly looked behind me, "That is the biggest damned crow I have ever seen."

I slowly turned and sure enough a black as midnight crow was sitting on the lodge pole railing of the corral not ten yards behind me. An overwhelming sense of dread came over me looking at this messenger sent from the "Great Spirit." After several seconds of trying to figure what the crow's presence meant, I heard in the distance Walk With Ghost as she yelled out, "MATT LEE!"

Looking over Spirit's saddle back down the main street of Grand Lake toward the Lake Saloon, I could see that Walk With Ghost was struggling with one of three U.S. Cavalry soldiers on the boardwalk in front of the saloon. He had his arms around her waist and had pulled her face first into his chest area and was trying to kiss her as she struggled to break free.

Grabbing the reins on Spirit and mounting all in one swift motion, I turned my mare towards Walk With Ghost and gave Spirit some spur as she broke out in an all-out dead run.

CHAPTER 15

Just as I started in her direction, Walk With Ghost was able to free her right hand and reached up and clawed the soldier's face. And even from this distance I could see the blood start to well in what would be permanent scratches left on his face.

With blood dripping down his face, the wounded soldier pushed her savagely away as hard as he could and drew his Remington army issue pistol and aimed it at her after she landed on her behind in the street. At a full gallop I started to draw my Winchester from the saddle scabbard as the soldier pulled the trigger and shot Walk With Ghost.

Letting go of Spirit's reins and the mare knowing me well enough to keep racing down the street, I put my Winchester to my shoulder and fired once, then jacked a new shell in the firing chamber and fired again. Both found a home in the soldier with the torn face. The first one caught him in the throat and before he could react the second found a home in his face doing way more damage than Walk With Ghost did.

Spirit made up the distance in record time and I dismounted even before she came to a complete stop. As soon as my feet hit the ground just short of where Walk With Ghost was lying in the street, the other two soldiers came out of the momentary shock and started to draw their sidearms.

I had closed the distance to the closest soldier before his pistol cleared leather. Dropping my Winchester and pulling my Bowie knife from its leather scabbard on my belt, I rushed in and met the soldier chest to chest, stabbing twice in his chest and then a quick and furious slice to his throat. Now showered with the dead man's blood, I held him upright and spun around, still holding the dead soldier as If he was a shield towards the third soldier left on the boardwalk who by that time had managed to clear leather with his pistol.

The third soldier fired twice in the back of his dead friend as I shoved the dead soldier in the direction of the third soldier. The third soldier had to back step to get out of the way of the soldier with his throat slit as the body started to fall in his direction which gave me time to palm my Colt and fire twice, and both found a home in the chest of the third soldier.

After the soldier had shot Walk With Ghost, it took no more than twenty seconds to dispatch the three soldiers on the boardwalk. It was twenty seconds too late.

I quickly reloaded my pistol and kept a close eye on the Lake Saloon expecting more adversaries from the Colorado 3rd Calvary to come out through the bat wing doors. I bent down and could see that Walk With Ghost was grimacing from the pain of being shot in her right shoulder, but very much still alive.

Speaking in a level tone to Walk With Ghost, "Hold on girl, I will get you some help shortly. I may have more soldier blue and yellow to deal with yet."

Just as I finished saying that, the remaining six soldiers slowly emerged from the bat wing doors of the saloon and walked out onto the boardwalk and spread out with all facing me. They were all youngsters and all liquored up, armed with the standard six shooters in leather flap holsters. The one on the far right, I could see it in his eyes, was the dumb one which made him the most dangerous - too stupid to know better and drunk to boot.

Slowly standing over Walk With Ghost, I knew I had a full load of six shells in my Colt, which was the exact number of hostile soldiers in front of me. The odds were not in my favor in this engagement. The flaps would slow them down some when they drew their weapons which, if it had been only two or three, would have been sufficient for me to come out the victor in any gunplay, but six was going to be almost impossible for me to survive. I had to survive for Walk With Ghost; she needed my help in a big way.

The drunken dumb one on the right said in a not too pleasant voice, "Old man you shot our friends over a squaw. What in the hell is wrong with you? They were just playing around."

Looking him straight in the eye, but still watching the others, I said in a very calm voice, "She is my wife and no man touches her. I mean no man and if you say squaw one more time boy, I will kill you where you stand."

Feeling brave in numbers the far right soldier said, "Can you count old man? There are six of us and one of you."

Smiling and with confidence in my voice, "There used to be nine of you, and I have whittled it down some. As I see it, the two on the far left are too scared to draw. The next three may or may not draw, but it really does not matter much, because when the slugs start to fly, my first shot is…you son. Now I am tired of this talk and either you apologize to me and my wife or draw that pistol. Those are your only two options so choose wisely."

He was going to go for his pistol; he was too stupid not to. Just as I thought that, he started and once again I palmed my Colt and shot him dead center of his chest. I moved my Colt in lightning speed to begin the play against the remaining five. To the man, all five never went for their guns and raised their hands above their waist.

The awkward silence and tension was broken as I faced the five soldiers as I felt the cold steel of a pistol barrel pressed against the back of my neck. Then a voice I recognized spoke from behind me, "There has been enough killing today Matt Lee. I can't let you kill the rest of these youngsters."

With Marshal Robert's pistol still pressed to my skull, I replied calmly, "All the fight has left these soldier boys; there is no more fight left in them."

With his Colt still pointed at the back of my head, Marshal Eric Robert spoke to the five soldiers still with their hands raised above their waists, "My name is Eric Robert and I am the duly appointed Territorial Marshal in this part of Colorado. Now you remaining soldiers go back into the saloon and find a place to plant your butt until I come take your statements. And if any of you even peek outside those bat wing doors, I am liable to shoot you myself. Do I make myself clear?"

All five seemed almost relieved to be able to walk away from this shooting scrape without getting plugged. They filed back into the saloon without saying a word.

With the soldiers now safely tucked away in the Lake Saloon, Marshal Robert said to the back of my head, "Now Matt Lee I need you to drop your Colt."

Shaking my head slowly in the motion of a "no," I spoke still with a calm voice, "You better pull that trigger Marshal; I am not giving up my gun for no man, even if he is a Territorial Marshal. I did nothing wrong here today except defend my wife's honor and our lives. That soldier blue shot my wife and he and the others paid the ultimate price for that. What I can promise you Marshal Robert is that I will re-holster my Colt and get the help my wife desperately needs right now. I have no fight with you or the law right now."

A few seconds passed before I no longer felt the pressure of a pistol barrel and heard the sound of the Marshal putting his Colt in his holster. "You know Matt Lee I get the feeling you can be a real asshole when you want to be."

Dropping my Colt back into my holster, I heard Walk With Ghost trying to lighten the mood with the pained reply to the Marshal, "That he can be Marshal, that he can be."

Slowly more of the Grand Lake town folks started to come outside. Always after a gunfight a large crowd would gather to see who lived and who died. Grand Lake was no different than any other town in the Rocky Mountains.

As I tended to my wife, Marshal Robert called to a couple of freighters that were standing next to their empty wagon to bring it over to transport Walk With Ghost to get some doctoring.

As the Marshal and I loaded Walk With Ghost into the back of the wagon, we looked each other in the eye, and we both knew that the events that had happened here today were not the end of it. That fate may in the future pit us against each other on opposite sides of a gun.

If that day happened, it would sadden me because I actually respected and liked the Marshal and I could see it in his eyes he felt the same way.

With no real doctor in town, we headed the wagon back to the Baldwin Hotel. I hoped that Walk with Ghost and I were still welcomed there after the gloomy events of the day.

CHAPTER 16

A ny misgiving about Sherol Roy and Roger Baldwin making Walk With Ghost or myself feel unwelcome after what just happened on the streets of Grand Lake, was quickly dismissed as we were met with open arms and concern for Walk With Ghost.

Sherol Roy indicated which room to put Walk With Ghost in and Marshal Robert and I laid her gently onto a bed that Sherol had quickly prepared for my wife.

Having done that, the Marshal made a quick exit without saying one word to me. I assumed he was heading back to the Lake Saloon to begin an investigation into the shooting.

It was not long after examining the wound that I was confident it was not life threatening since the bullet had passed through and through and had missed the collar bone. There was an ample amount of blood loss, of course, but as far as Sherol Roy and I could see, none of the major rivers that pumped blood to the heart had been severed. Walk With Ghost was tougher than most and would be laid up for a spell, but should recover fully. After cleaning the wound completely, Sherol applied some pine needle salve to both the entrance and exit wounds. After the doctoring, Walk With Ghost was understandably exhausted and was able to fall into a deep sleep.

Sherol Roy made some coffee for both Roger and me, and we sat at the dining room table as I gathered my thoughts on what I believed would happen next.

Sherol Roy, because she was a gracious and kind woman, replied, "Walk With Ghost and you are more than welcome to stay here free of charge until she is fully recovered so you can continue your journey to your Redemption Valley. I would guess she might be able to travel in three to four weeks."

Roger wholeheartedly agreed that was the correct action to take. Being the good and righteous people that they were, Sherol Roy and Roger Baldwin did not understand that the military and the rest of the townsfolk were more than likely not going to look favorably on the fact that I had just killed four troopers over an incident with an Indian. In most whites' eyes, my wife Walk With Ghost was held in disdain and would be looked down on that she was some animal lower than some mangy mutt.

Hearing some commotion and voices from outside, I palmed my Colt and went to the window facing the main road to Grand Lake and pulled back the curtain just far enough to be able to look through the broad glass window.

Peering through the window, I saw the Colorado 3rd marching into town. They did not have the look as if they had been in any battle and I took this to mean that Chief Piah and the renegades had agreed to head to the reservation over in Utah.

The whole troop was being led by none other than Master Sergeant Andy Cacy and that weasel 1st Lieutenant Art Wilson. Master Sergeant Cacy happened to look my way and saw me and simply nodded in my direction. I returned his nod with misgivings since they obviously did not know as of yet I had just killed four of their own.

Sitting back down, I made sure my Winchester and Colt were fully loaded. Not that I wanted to battle a full troop of U.S. Cavalry troopers, but if it came down to it, the "Ghost" in me would give them everything I had and then some. My sole reason for living was to protect my wife lying wounded in the other room, and she was not fit to travel. Nothing else mattered; she was why I was saved that day at that distant mountain pond. If I had to make a stand and die trying, so be it.

Turning to Sherol Roy and Roger Baldwin, "Listen to me very carefully, I know the good folks that you are and will not understand why, but I assure you the soldiers will be coming for me soon and you cannot be here when they do. I wish the Lord would have seen fit not to have this happen here in your home and place of business, but I did not choose this. You must leave and leave now, your lives will be in jeopardy if you stay."

Sherol was confused and baffled, but Roger understood and he went to a cabinet in the living room and grabbed his Winchester and a Greener 12 gauge shotgun with all the ammo he had and laid them on the kitchen table. Looking at me as he grabbed Sherol's arm to hustle her out the door, he said, "Best I can do Matt Lee, just know when the dust settles, if needed we will look after Walk With Ghost."

Reaching out to shake his hand in a firm handshake, "You are a good man Roger, and one to ride the river with. Now you get the hell out of here and get your wife to safety."

After Sherol Roy and Roger left their home, I tried to size up the Baldwin Hotel to see how easy it would be to defend. It only took a few seconds to realize this was possibly the worst case scenario to defend - too many windows and the lodge pine construction would burn easily, but with no time to move Walk With Ghost to a better location, this would have to do.

The thought did cross my mind about taking the fight to the street and the outside and fight them in the elements. That was more suited for my type of guerilla warfare. I quickly dismissed that idea because it would leave Walk With Ghost all alone and if we both were going to die today, we needed to be together. Fate had dealt the cards this way and live or die I had to play this hand out to the end. There would be no fold in the "Ghost."

I went in and checked on Walk With Ghost, and she was still sleeping soundly. I kept the door open so I would be able to see her with just a glance.

Moving to the window and looking out the broad glass, I saw a lone rider moving at a fast trot my way. It was Marshal Eric Robert.

Dismounting, he saw me in the window and he spoke loud enough for me to hear, "I am coming in Matt Lee, we need to talk."

I went over and sat down at the table facing the door and laid the 12 gauge Greener shotgun on top of the table next to my Winchester with the barrel facing the door and Marshal Robert as soon as he walked through the door.

The Marshal slowly opened the door and when it was fully opened, I noticed his Colt was still in its holster. He did not come to fight me, not this time anyway. Stepping in, he pulled up a chair across from me at the table and slowly moved the barrel of the shotgun away so it was not pointed at his chest, "I see you are ready to make a stand. I had not thought of you as a shotgun man."

With calm in my voice, "I am not, but Roger being the good man that he is, left it for me thinking I may need it. You did not come here to remark on the ins and outs of using a shotgun to kill a man. What do you want Marshal?"

Straight to the point the Marshal began, "You must have seen the whole Colorado 3rd as they rode by. Their commanding officer, a 1st Lieutenant named Art Wilson, is claiming to have military jurisdiction over this matter since it was his troopers you killed. He is asking everyone where you might have gone and no one is talking, but it won't be long before he starts a house to house search. You and I both know they will not take you alive. His trooper shooting your wife means nothing to them since she is an Indian. And realizing the man that you are, you will not leave your wife here because she is too wounded to travel, so you will feel cornered, and you will fight to the death. So…that being said, since no formal warrant for your arrest has been handed down from a territorial court, and I see this as justified shooting, I would like to prevent any further bloodshed and it would make my day for you to ride out of here before they find you. And hopefully I can clear this damn mess up."

Thinking that Master Sergeant Andy Cacy had seen me as they rode by and had said nothing to his superior told me all I needed to know about the Master Sergeant. It didn't take him long to figure out what really happened. Pondering everything the Marshal had said, I responded, "It all comes down to Walk With Ghost cannot travel, so I make my stand here. I will not abandon her to those that would rather see her dead."

The Marshal's eyes told me he understood, "What if I personally guaranteed her safety until she was well enough to travel."

Before I could respond, Walk With Ghost spoke out from the bedroom, "Matt Lee, come talk to me and bring the Marshal."

Both the Marshal and I made our way to the bedroom and Walk With Ghost was wide awake but in obvious pain. Sitting gently on the edge of the bed, I held her hand as she spoke, "I heard the whole conversation and you must trust my gut instinct, and I believe Marshal Robert when he says he will keep me safe. If we are to ever make Redemption Valley our last home, you need to live beyond today. You must go now. Your wanderings in the past have taken you away from me before, and I am use to it. When I am well enough to travel, come back and get me and hopefully this mess with the Cavalry will be just a distant memory. Promise me Matt Lee that you will leave and live."

Looking at Walk With Ghost's pleading eyes, I knew she was correct. And I believed the Marshal when he said he would guarantee her safety; dying today would serve no purpose. Shaking my head "yes" and squeezing her hand a little tighter before I spoke, "I also believe the Marshal so I agree, but I will be back and take my love to our Redemption Valley."

After bending over to kiss my wife on her lips. I lingered and spoke softly for only her to hear, "I was blessed the day you entered my life and on this day I realize how lucky I truly have been to have you and our love and to have this difficulty in saying goodbye."

Walk With Ghost's eyes filled with tears and showed her love when she said, "Just go Matt Lee, leave now and don't look back. I am having a tough time holding back the tears. Hurry, my love."

Leaving the bedroom I did not look back, for I did not want to show Walk With Ghost my tears.

Marshal Robert followed me to the door and as I picked up my Winchester, he grabbed my arm to stop me and we locked eyes. "Understand Matt Lee, my promise to you is that I will protect your wife with my life if it comes to that. You must also understand if the territorial court should issue a warrant for your arrest, it is my sworn duty to serve it. I will come looking for you."

Still with our eyes locked as only two men that someday may meet on the battlefield can, "I respect you Marshal, and I sense you are a good man and I am beholden to you for looking after to make sure Walk With Ghost is safe. And if a warrant is issued, I do understand your honor and obligation to try and serve it. You must also understand if such a warrant is issued, it is my death warrant, because the military will hang me for killing those troopers if they deserved it or not. I will not let you or the 3rd Cavalry stop me from taking my wife to our home in Redemption Valley. I will die in the quest before I let you take me in. Just so we both understand each other."

Marshal Eric Robert shook his head "yes" and then let go of my arm, "Understood Matt Lee, now get the hell out of here."

Stepping into the stirrup to mount Spirit, I left Sky for Walk With Ghost. Reining Spirit to the west, I gave her a slight jab of the spur and she took off at a fast trot out of Grand Lake.

CHAPTER 17

K nowing that the U.S. Cavalry was on the lookout for me, I stayed off the well-traveled trails and took to the timber. It would be slower going, but Spirit was a one of a kind mountain horse and was used to the rough terrain. She seemed to enjoy the physical workout and the challenge of walking the dark timber provided. Patting her neck, I spoke softly to her, "Going to be this way for a spell I reckon and I know how you like it. It is that wild side of you that gets the chance to show itself."

Spirit lifted her head twice and snorted. She knows things had changed since Walk With Ghost and Sky were not with us. She was almost human with her natural ability to reason things out. Spirit had a more gut instinct than most humans had.

Since the whole Colorado 3rd had showed up in Grand Lake and looking healthy to boot, I assumed that Chief Piah and his renegades had decided to head to the reservation without a fight. No way, no how did I want Walk With Ghost's brother hearing of his sister being shot by a U.S. Cavalry trooper. He would turn the

Middle Park Basin into a bloody battlefield that would serve no purpose whatsoever. In the 30 plus years of knowing the man, I could predict exactly how he thinks.

To stay well hidden from any roaming U.S. Cavalry patrols, I decided to head to the remote timber of the Kawuneeche Valley north of where the Ute renegades had wintered. I had my doubts that any of the young troopers would have that much skill in woodcraft that they would be able to track me, but you never knew.

Since it was spring time, it would be easier to snare enough smaller critters such as rabbits or squirrels for food than having to use my guns to bring down a deer or an elk. I did not want to have a rifle report give away my location.

I would have to move my campsite every two days trying not to establish a pattern of coming and going to one spot and I would stay well-hidden and away from anyone that might be searching for me. I had learned my woodcraft skill long ago when I was "Ghost" and those skills kept me alive then and they would do so now. The difference now was that I did not have the madness sickness; I did not have the rage and chaos from those years. My sole purpose and concern was to wait long enough for Walk With Ghost to heal enough to be able to travel. I was hopeful that the Marshal Eric Robert would be able to convince the powers to be that it was a righteous and justified killing of the four troopers. But, in my heart, I knew that would never come about since it all started over a trooper trying to steal a kiss from an Indian.

Thinking back on what my reaction was to the incident, I had no regrets. That trooper treated my wife as if she was nothing at all, a non-human. I will not tolerate bad behavior in man toward my wife nor anyone else for that matter. If a man did not defend the honor of his wife, then he was no man at all. I did not want an all-out war against the U.S. government and its military as I did 30 years ago against the Utes, but a man had to draw a line somewhere.

All I wanted was to spend the remainder of my years with Walk With Ghost in Redemption Valley. But the good Lord has seen fit to put as many obstacles in my way as possible. There is no giving up in me and if I have to fight my way to our valley, then so be it. Looking toward the heavens and the man that resided there, I spoke in a loud clear voice, "Give me an open road to the Redemption Valley Lord, or I will summon the demon that resides within me and bring Hell along for the ride."

The weeks went by painfully slow and I was getting antsy to head back south to Grand Lake for some information and to see if Walk With Ghost had healed up enough to travel. Spirit was also anxious to be back on the trail; she was a horse born in the wild to travel the wilderness trails.

The night of the beginning of the third week since the shooting, I was awakened by Spirit snorting loudly and grabbed my six shooter from under my saddle which I had been using to lay my head at night. It wasn't long before I realized it was not man nor beast that had spooked my mare, but only a falling star.

My fire was almost out with just the last of the orange glow of the embers fading fast. It was darkness that engulfed the nearby evergreens and aspens. It was the sky that was lit for all to see as the falling star seemed to burn a brilliant white light in the heavens.

I had seen only a handful in my lifetime and I knew this to be a rare event. This one seemed to take much longer than the ones I had witnessed earlier in my life. It had started in the southern sky and made its way to the north on this cloudless and quarter moon night. I watched the arc as it made tracks across the midnight sky until it faded in the north going to parts unknown. It was seeing such things as this that made me love the wilderness and realize in the grand scheme of things that I and everyone else that called this earth home were really just here for a blink of an eye. We are born, we live, we die, we become dust in the wind, and I was okay with that.

For some reason seeing the falling star seemed like a sign from heaven that I needed to get back on the trail and head to Grand Lake come first light.

After a hearty breakfast of roasted rabbit and the last of the beans from my supplies, I filled my canteens with fresh creek water and packed the rest of my meager belongings into my saddle bags and a bedroll.

I took the time to clean and oil my weapons and loaded my Colt with six shells instead of the normal five. When traveling, I would usually keep the cylinder under the hammer empty for safety, but times were different now. I would have to assume that the U.S. Cavalry was my enemy at this point and needed to be fully loaded in my Winchester and Colt.

I also took the time to rub down Spirit and feed her the last of my grain that I had. She lifted her head twice expecting sugar, but with what happened on the streets of Grand Lake, the sugar for her treats was lost that day due to more pressing matters. Spirit seemed to be a tad cranky about that outcome. I gave her ears some extra loving to make up for it. Didn't work though, she was still cranky without her sugar. Sometimes trying to understand Spirit was like trying to understand any female condition and I was lacking enough meat in the brain pan to make any sense of it all. I gave her neck a hug anyway before I saddled her.

It would take two days of traveling just on the inside edge of the dark timber and sticking to the shadows to make it back to Grand Lake. Moving slowly and silently was the task at hand now. I could not do anything to make myself and Spirit stand out so others that may be hunting me would take notice.

It was on the second day that I noticed movement on the trail heading south to Grand Lake. Still mounted on Spirit, but well hidden in the shadows, I took out my newfangled Porro prism binoculars which were named after some Italian fellow named Ignazio Porro. Chance had given them to me as a present for saving his life last winter.

What I saw with perfect clarity were twenty "green as grass" troopers being led by none other than Master Sergeant Andy Cacy heading north. It would seem after three weeks after the renegades had left the area that there was still a military presence in Grand Lake and the Middle Park Basin, which meant the U.S. Cavalry still had a mission to fulfill. Now I was never schooled in the "going to school" type way, but that didn't mean I couldn't read, write, and decipher. I didn't have to be a book learner to realize that more than likely I was their mission. Just as I thought, they were not taking kindly to my killing four of the boys in blue and yellow.

The troopers were heading north and keeping to the well-worn trails like I would be foolish enough to ride down one of those. Master Sergeant Andy Cacy should know better; then again, maybe he did. I got the feeling he knew the true score of what happened that day and probably was not putting in a full hearted attempt to find me. I kept thinking back to that day he saw me in the window and did not tell that weasel 1st Lieutenant of his my location.

Giving Spirit a slight jab of my spur, I urged her south and away from the troopers towards Grand Lake and what awaited us there.

CHAPTER 18

F inding a spot that was suitable up on the mountain and in the timber and the shadows met my need of remaining hidden; furthermore, it gave me a good view to observe the comings and goings of Grand Lake and the Baldwin Hotel.

The days and nights so far this spring had been warm with chilly nights, but no severe weather of any kind. Today was no different from those that had passed in the last three weeks.

There was a lot of troop activity in town still - which was not very good news to me. Looking at the front porch of the Baldwin through my Italian binoculars at mid-afternoon, I spotted another bit of bad news. Marshal Eric Robert stepped out and sat down to enjoy his pipe. It was obvious from his casual manner today that he was still staying at the hotel. The question was whether his current mission was to still keep the troopers in line in Grand Lake or that there had been a warrant issued for me? Rolling it around in my mind some, I knew it could also mean both.

Observing from afar was giving me more questions than answers. Sooner or later I was just going to have to ride down there and ask someone, "What the hell is going on?"

The front door slowly opened and Sherol Roy stood holding the door for a minute as Walk With Ghost slowly joined her on the front porch and took a seat on the far end away from the Marshal. When she turned her face to soak in some sun, it reminded me of the very first day I saw her at that distant pond. My heart skipped a beat just as it did on that day over 30 years ago. There was no doubt after all these years I still loved that woman just as much as the first day I saw her.

The good news was that Walk With Ghost was up and around, but she seemed to be taking it slowly which indicated she was still on the mend. My wife is one tough and strong woman. I could not think of one woman that I have ever known that could take a 44 slug and just three weeks later would be taking coffee on the front porch.

Looking to the west, I saw a lone rider approaching and even though the rider was too far away to see the face, I knew who it was by his horse. Only one man rode a horse like this in the whole Rocky Mountain frontier and the horse was an Appaloosa mare named Cimarron and was almost as famous as the rider.

Cimarron was an Appaloosa Gruella mare with white spots over back and hips. Her facial markings consisted of a white as snow star in between the eyes and a white snip below the top of the nostrils. And her hind legs both had partial white socks. And of course she had the mottled skin around her mouth and the Appaloosa trait of striped hooves. What set her aside from other Appaloosa mares was she was bigger than most at almost 19 hands tall and heavily muscled and a stamina second to none. I heard a story once that she rode at a fast trot for two days straight without tiring or floundering. Of course she was also a man killer having killed two men on two different occasions that had tried to steal her from her owner by kicking them to death. Her owner was none other than the famed bounty hunter Doug Webb.

Doug Webb came out of the civil war after fighting for the south with a reputation as a sniper and of a man that liked to kill in hand-to-hand combat. Doug was younger than I was by about 15 years, but had a full head of hair roughly the same color as mine of almost pure white. He was big and heavily muscled at about 6'3" and weighed about 230 or so. Webb came out of the war with some deadly skills and had become a man hunter for money. He was known to be dangerous with a bowie knife or tomahawk, but he also wore the standard Colt 44 that most men on the frontier wore. It was said that he was a fast draw with his Colt, - maybe not as fast as Lucas Eldridge, Johnny Ringo, or even Chance Bondurant - but still fast. Webb was a killer and not a likeable man and he was more apt to shoot you in the back if he could. I was once present in Sheridan, Colorado when Webb showed up with Troy Cummins the bank robber to collect his bounty, not the body of Cummins, just his severed head in a gunny sack.

The only reason the man killer and his horse were now riding towards Grand Lake was that he was looking to earn a bounty. That could only mean one thing and that was sometime in the last three weeks a bounty had been placed on my head and for a bounty hunter like Webb to come here, it had to be a substantial one. Bounty hunter Doug Webb and his man killer horse Cimarron were not to be trifled with.

Grabbing a half pound of elk jerky and my canteen of water, I ate a cold meal as I started to ponder my next move. Troopers Eric Robert and Doug Webb were all present and accounted for in Grand Lake. Even though that all seemed to be bad news for me, but without hearing it or experiencing it first hand, I really did not know what it all meant.

All I know is that my original plans had not changed. It would seem that Walk With Ghost either was or would be close enough to travel and we were going to our Redemption Valley and disappear from those that wished to harm us. Simple…yes; doable…that was yet to be determined.

Howard Smith, the owner of the livery, seemed like a man that I could trust, and I had a feeling the man was hiding from something deep in his past and would not want to draw attention to himself. I reckoned he was a man I could find the answers to what was going on in Grand Lake in regards to the Marshal, bounty hunter, U.S. Cavalry, and of course myself.

Taking Spirit's reins, I tied her off to a tree so she would not wander. Thinking I should visit Mr. Smith about midnight tonight, I better get some shut eye now. Lying down in the high mountain grass under Spirit to sleep, I knew she would keep me safe and warn me in plenty of time in case someone would happen my way.

Waking up I remained still and not moving for several minutes listening to the sounds of the night trying to hear anything out of kilter from what it should be. Hearing none, I spoke quietly to Spirit, "Moving out from underneath you girl. Don't step on me now."

By the half-moon's position I could tell it was about midnight and thought it was time to make a visit to Howard Smith at the livery stable. When I was there before three weeks ago, I had noticed he had living quarters next to the tack room and it was obvious that was where Mr. Smith lived.

After saddling and mounting Spirit, I once again listened to the night sounds and let my eyes adjust to the dark. The sky was cloudless with countless stars blinking in the night sky. The mountain air had a slight chill to it with no breeze or movement of any kind. The smell of budding aspens and lodge pole pine scented the air - which I liked. I could also smell wood smoke from the numerous cooking fires that had burned this evening.

Riding east slowly so as not to make a sound, I rode just inside the timberline up and behind the town of Grand Lake until I was directly behind the livery stable. Dismounting and tying off Spirit to an evergreen branch, I reached in my saddle bag to gather my moccasins to wear.

As I made my way through the corral and horses, Walk With Ghost's mare Sky was excited to see me and snorted several times as she tossed her head a couple of times as she nudged me with her nose. I spent several minutes loving and speaking quietly to her to calm her down.

Working my way soundlessly into Howard Smith's room where he was fast asleep, I was able to remove his Colt from underneath his bed without disturbing him. Once I felt that I had all of his weapons out of his reach, I sat down in the chair across from Howard and pulled out my corn cob pipe. After packing it full of tobacco, I slid a stick match across the tabletop to light my pipe. The sound of the match igniting woke Howard out of a dead sleep as he reached for his Colt which was no longer there. Howard was startled and spoke loudly as he searched in vain for his pistol, "What the hell? Who the hell are you?"

Smiling and with a slight chuckle, I spoke to Howard as he tried to gain his bearings after rudely being woke up, "It is Matt Lee and I am Sorry Mr. Smith to barge in like this, but I reckon I could not come in the daylight."

Still startled and swinging his legs out to stand up and in failing to do so, Howard fell back hard onto his bunk, "For Christ sake Matt Lee I could have killed you!"

Chuckling more loudly this time, "For that to happen, you would have to be awake and armed with a weapon."

Finally seeing the absurdity of his statement, Howard started to laugh out loud and spread his hands out in a questioning manner, "I reckon so Matt Lee. What the hell happened to my pistol?"

Pulling on my pipe to get a lung full, I reached out and handed Howard his fully loaded pistol, "Here it is, and I just need to ask a few questions is all."

Howard was starting to wake up fully and took his pistol and checked to see if it was still loaded and laid it back down under the bed and then chuckled lightly as he said, "Guess I will have to find a better hidey hole from assholes like you. What can I do for you Mr. Lee?"

Still smiling I said, "I reckon you need to sleep a tad lighter also, Mr. Smith. To answer your question, I have not talked to any person since my shoot out with the soldiers and I have no idea what the lay of the land might be. I have my thoughts of course, but I need you to tell me what is what around here."

Howard stood up to stir the coals in his cast iron stove to get a flame going. After he had a flicker of flames, he added some wood, then moved his coffee pot onto the top to warm up some leftover coffee. "Might as well have a cup of brown gargle while we are jawing the night away. Right after you shot those soldier boy skunks for manhandling and shooting your wife, that no account 1st lieutenant Wilson showed up and got to bitching about how you shot up his boys for no reason. Somehow he was able to pull jurisdiction and he and most of the Colorado 3rd are still here about searching for you. It is no secret Matt Lee if they take you alive, they plan on hanging you.

The U.S. Cavalry went complaining down Denver way and got an arrest warrant issued by the territorial court for you with a dead or alive bounty of $2000. Now, Marshal Eric Robert spoke on your behalf in a telegram to Denver explaining the facts as he saw them, but it was to no avail. The warrant still stands. The Marshal seems like a reasonable man and seems in no hurry to try and serve that warrant on you.

The bad kicker here Matt Lee is that back shooting bounty hunter Doug Webb showed up today looking to start trailing you for the $2000."

Drawing another lung full from my pipe and taking the cup of coffee offered from Howard, "Much as I surmised Howard accepted the $2000, which is a lot of money. Has the thought crossed your mind to try and collect that yourself?"

Howard sat down with his cup warming both hands on the tin cup of coffee. "I would have to admit that $2000 is more money than I have ever seen in my life, but I reckon there are a couple things worth more than money. First one is in my eyes you did nothing wrong other than protect your wife's honor and I admire that. The second reason is I would prefer not to tangle with a man that can sneak up on you and take your pistol whilst you are sleeping. The third reason is for reasons that are my own; I do not want to draw attention to myself here in Grand Lake. I like my quiet life here and make a decent enough of a living to keep me happy."

Having gathered as much information that I was going to get, I drank half the cup of coffee, stood up, and reached out to shake Howard's hand, "I would like to pay the tab on Sky for her keep."

Howard shakes my hand, "No need because Roger Baldwin paid for her a month in advance. You have good friends here in Grand Lake Matt Lee."

Letting go of Howard's hand, "Friends enough to keep my visit quiet here this evening?"

Laughing Howard said, "I have no idea who the hell you are mister."

Walking out of Howard's living quarters, I thought of one last thing to say to Howard and turning toward him with a smile, "Thanks for the information and the coffee. Not sure if you are aware, but your coffee tastes like shit."

Howard laughed out loud, "I reckon I am not much of a coffee cooker."

CHAPTER 19

F eeling that Howard Smith was a man of honor and would keep his word and not mention that I was in Grand Lake, and since most of the night had already passed and the dawn was a couple of hours away, I would wait until tonight to get Walk With Ghost and make our way to our Redemption Valley.

My observation point overlooking the Baldwin Hotel that I used yesterday would be the best possible place to wait out the coming daylight hours and catch some much needed shut eye. I had a feeling that once Walk With Ghost and I left Grand Lake, it would be a race and possible deadly one at that making our way to Redemption Valley on the eastern side of the "Great Divide" above Como on Boreas Pass.

While it was still dark I tied off Spirit, unsaddled her, and then crawled underneath her again to get some sleep. Listening in the dark to the after midnight sounds and hearing nothing unusual, I fell asleep.

Waking at dawn after only a few hours of sleep, I grabbed some elk jerky for another cold meal and drank heavily from my canteen. Keeping my binoculars close in case anything unusual should happen in or around the Baldwin Hotel, I began to ponder once I had my wife what the next move in our journey would be.

I thought of the terrain and the difficulties we would encounter as we made our trip of roughly 110 miles to the east side of Boreas Pass from Grand Lake.

Such a trip would normally be a five to seven day journey in the spring and early summer weather. This trip, however, would take much longer since the U.S. Cavalry, Marshal Robert, and now Doug Webb the bounty hunter would be trying to trail me. U.S. Cavalry more likely than not would be doing it for revenge for my killing four of their own; Marshal Robert because it was his sworn duty; and Doug Webb for the dead or alive bounty of $2000.

The trip would consist of some very difficult terrain since we would cross numerous rivers and mountain passes, not to mention we would have to cross the "Great Divide" twice during our flight south to our hidden valley and home in Redemption Valley.

The thought had crossed my mind that it had been many years since I was in the valley that Walk With Ghost and I had earmarked as our new home far from those that would want to do us harm. Hopefully no one had claimed the lost valley for their own since then. Of course that was a possibility I had to consider and having decided not to waste any of my thinking time on something I could not change without more information, I pushed it into the back of my mind.

The morning activity in Grand Lake seemed to be just the normal comings and goings of such a supply depot and nothing seemed out of kilter. Marshal Robert took his coffee on the porch and did not seem to be in any hurry to go anywhere. He was a smart man and realized I was coming there to get Walk With Ghost sooner or later. This was a confrontation I would prefer not to have since I respected the man and his badge and his sense of duty. Being the man that the Marshal was, he also knew I would not hesitate in doing what needed to be done to get my wife.

In my observation on this sunny spring morning, I also noticed two U.S. Cavalry troops of ten soldiers each moving westward out of town. They were loaded down with their bedrolls and saddle bags meaning they would be gone for a prolonged time. I could only assume they were searching for me. I had no indication that the bounty hunter Doug Webb was in town and that bothered me some not knowing where he was.

Sitting up here on the mountain north of the Baldwin Hotel, I could not see the Colorado River, but I know its course well enough and would have no problem locating it in the dark tonight so Walk With Ghost and I could follow it.

The Colorado River started several miles north of my position at the La Poudre Pass Lake just at timberline at a little over 10,000 feet. It started just as a trickle and flowed south and became slightly larger until it started to flow southwest across the Middle Park Basin.

After leaving Grand Lake, we would stay in the dark timber that ran along the Colorado River's banks traveling roughly 16 miles until we reached the Fraser River which started at the top of Berthoud Pass and flowed northwest until it ran into the Colorado.

Once we found the Fraser River, we would then follow it up stream southeast across the Middle park basin country to Berthoud Pass which was another 16 or so miles.

Berthoud was a high mountain pass that topped out on top of the world about 1000 feet above where the trees never grow and the snow never melts. It was one that I have traversed several times in the past. "The Great Divide" would be the first pass that we would have to cross on our journey to Redemption Valley. Even though the Ute Indians had been using the pass since their time began, the first white man to cross over was none other than the famed mountain man and explorer Jim Bridger almost twenty years ago. Several years later, Bridger would be back to the pass with Edward L. Berthoud, the chief surveyor of the Colorado Central Railroad. Not sure of the reasoning, but the pass was named after Berthoud instead of Bridger. Berthoud concluded that the pass was suitable as a wagon road, but not as a railroad so the idea to run tracks over the lofty pass was abandoned.

Once over Berthoud Pass we would be able to follow Fall River until it reached Clear Creek in Clear Creek Canyon. We then of course would follow Clear Creek upstream to the mining camp of Georgetown which sat at the bottom of Guanella Pass which would be an additional 19 to 20 miles.

Georgetown and the town just a mile to the northwest Silver Plume had been silver mining towns that were discovered after the Peaks Peak gold rush. Georgetown was nestled into the northeast corner of Clear Creek Canyon.

Silver Plume, even though I had never been there, was famous for the shoot-out between my very good friend Lucas Eldridge and the Mexican bandit Juan Verdugo. Lucas killed Verdugo, but was severely wounded and was saved from an ambush by the bartender Bill Termes when the bartender took a hand in the fight and killed a relative of Verdugo that had the drop on Lucas with a 12 gauge shotgun blast. I intended to avoid Silver Plume at all cost since their sheriff Kurt Wollenweber was well known as a hard-nosed and honest lawman who was rumored to be almost as fast with his Colt as my friends Chance and Lucas. He was a man in my current status with the law that I did not want to have an encounter with.

Guanella Pass would be the second and the last pass over "The Great Divide" that Walk With Ghost and I would have to travel in our pursuit for our hidden valley. It also was a high mountain pass that was over 1000 feet above timberline and where summer never existed at those lordly heights.

From Georgetown over Guanella Pass into the valley of Geneva Creek and the tributary of the North Fork of South Platte River would be roughly 24 miles.

The summit of Kenosha Pass was about six miles southwest of the North Fork of the South Platte River.

Kenosha Pass at roughly 10,000 feet topped out just a tad below timberline and was not part of "The Great Divide" but part of the spine of mountains that formed the eastern side of South Park, another high mountain plateau basin much like Middle Park and their sister plateau basin many miles to the north of where I now found myself that was called North Park. "The person who named these basins, North, Middle, and South Parks must have had to work hard to get their thinking clean to make it simple," I chuckled to myself.

Once we reached the northeastern edge of South Park, it would be a quick dash of another 25 miles past the towns of Jefferson and Como and up the eastern side of Boreas Pass to our home in Redemption Valley.

Once I had our trail to Redemption Valley planted in my mind, I realized it would be a difficult or damn near impossible journey with so many wanting me arrested or dead. It was a journey and task I would not shy away from and was more than suited to complete. My whole life had been one constant battle for survival and I was ready. I knew Walk With Ghost saw it the same way I did, for we were more alike than she would care to admit.

Still having several hours of daylight to wait, I scooted back underneath Spirit to catch some more shut-eye.

CHAPTER 20

Waking up as soon as the sun dropped down below the top of the evergreen and aspens in the western horizon, I was once again awed by a typical glorious Rocky Mountain orange and blue sundown, and I will always marvel at the beauty of a high mountain end of the day and the beginning of the night. Being close to the heavens seems to make the colors of the end of day's sunset seem more alive and vibrant. Even at this point in time with so many wanting my head, I felt honored to have lived the bulk of my life in what had to be the Lord's garden. I could not imagine another place in the world that could match the Lord's and nature's handiwork in the high Rockies.

Grabbing some more elk jerky from my saddle bag, I ate as I rubbed down Spirit with a wooden curry comb, and she was enjoying the extra loving. I spoke to her gently of all things that were to come in the next several weeks and how much I was going to have to count on her to be strong in her strides and watchful for all of us with her keen hearing and eyesight to keep us safe as we tried to ride out of harm's way. Spirit rubbed her nose in a loving manner into my shoulder and neck as her way of telling me she understood. Spirit and Sky were horses like no other in the way they reacted to people. They seemed more in tune with me than I was with them.

As soon as it was dark and the moon had just started its nightly arc in the eastern sky, my first order of business was to get Sky from the livery stable. I followed the same path as before staying in the dark timber up on the mountain until I was directly behind the livery. Moving down alongside the corral, I noticed that Sky was already saddled with Walk With Ghost's saddle and all of the provisions that we had purchased on the day that Walk With Ghost was wounded.

Approaching the mare cautiously, I noticed a note pinned to the saddle. Grabbing the note, but keeping alert to all that was around me, I read it in the low light and it was a simple affair, "My way of making up for the coffee. If you are ever back this way again, you can buy me a bottle of whiskey." And it was signed simply HS. Smiling and tipping my hat to the livery stable, tack room, and the man sleeping within, I knew Howard Smith was one to ride the river with and I was proud to call him my friend.

Taking Sky's reins, I tied them to Spirit's saddle and began moving from north to south in crossing the main street of Grand Lake to get into the timber on the south side of town. Having reached the timber and the shadows of the trees, I moved slowly until I was directly behind the Baldwin Hotel.

Stepping out of the saddle, I moved with stealth toward the back of the hotel and when I was within a couple of yards, I could smell the smoke of someone smoking a pipe. Following the smoke, I walked around the side of the hotel and neared the front porch where the smoke was coming from.

Marshal Eric Robert was sitting on the front porch all by himself enjoying his pipe. His back was to the railing on the side of the porch that I was on. Drawing my Colt, I eased up on the Marshal and stuck the barrel of my pistol against the back of his neck, "Doesn't feel too good does it Marshal?"

Marshal Robert stiffened up as the cold steel was pressed against his neck, "No, it doesn't Matt Lee. I didn't figure you for the back shooting type."

Talking calmly and quietly for only the Marshal to hear, "Are you armed? If so, I need you to lay your weapon and any and all weapons on the floor in front of you. I would prefer not to kill you Marshal Robert, but they can only hang me once so one more death is not going to sway any judge one way or the other."

Marshal Robert responded, "The only thing I am armed with is my corn cob pipe and my witty demeanor this evening."

With my pistol still on the Marshal, I finished walking around to the front steps and made my way up onto the front porch. Once on the front porch, I indicated with the barrel of my pistol for the Marshal to stand up so we could enter the hotel, "Witty demeanor? I like that, I really do."

Once inside Sherol Roy and Roger were playing cribbage at the dinner table and Walk With Ghost was sitting next to Sherol watching the game progress. Pointing to the rocking chair in the great room, I indicated with my pistol again for the Marshal to take a seat which he promptly did.

Walk with Ghost and Sherol Roy jumped up and rushed over to give me a hug. Sherol noticed I had my pistol drawn and was pointing it at the Marshal when she put her hands on her hips and a frown crossed her face as she said, "Matt Lee put the pistol away! And you Marshal Eric Robert know better than to smoke in the hotel, now extinguish that pipe right now!"

It may be a do or die situation for the Marshal and me, but by damn this was Sherol Roy's home and while we were in it, she ruled the roost. Locking my eyes with the Marshal's, we both rolled them at the same time, which was our silent truce and understanding that nothing between the two of us was going to happen in these good folks' home and business. I holstered my pistol and Marshal Robert put out his corn cob pipe as we were told.

As Walk With Ghost rolled into my arms, I could hear Roger from the dinner table chuckle and say, "See boys what I have to put up with," which brought laughter from Roger, Sherol, and Walk With Ghost and a nervous chuckle from both the Marshal and myself.

After establishing the pecking order in the house, Sherol Roy said, "You must be starved Matt Lee. I got some roasted turkey and taters that I could warm up for you?"

Smiling, I said, "I could do with a good meal Sherol and it would be much appreciated."

Walk With Ghost was all smiles as she held on to me as if she never wanted to let go. Looking at this woman whom I loved more than anything, I caught myself smiling when I realized how much I had missed her these last several weeks and could not be here to help as she recovered. "Are you well enough to travel? It will have to be fast and furious."

Walk With Ghost as she headed to the bedroom, she spoke over her shoulder, "Been packed and ready for a week."

Sherol set up a plate of turkey and taters next to Roger, and I sat down facing the Marshal as he sat in the rocking chair. We locked eyes once again as we both tried to get a feeling of what the future held for the both of us.

The Marshal spoke first, "You know it is my job and sworn duty to serve this arrest warrant that has been issued by the territorial court. We spoke of this before. I am curious - what are your thoughts?"

Walk With Ghost joined me at the table and her faced showed concern, because she could feel the mounting tension between the Marshal and myself. Looking at her then back towards the Marshal, "I know you have a job to fulfill and right now that job is me. I know you are a good man and I am much obliged to your looking out for Walk With Ghost in my absence. I got this feeling you are going to be a pain in the ass and one of us is going to end up dead, so my gut instinct is to shoot you in the leg to hobble you some."

Marshal Eric Robert shrugged his shoulders as he thought about that prospect. "You must know by now you have way more trouble than me and the law. The Colorado 3rd Cavalry's sole mission at this present time is to find you and bring you back to trial and if you fight them, they have orders to shoot to kill. Then of course every bounty hunter in the Rocky Mountain frontier is looking to make that $2000 bounty that the courts have placed in a dead or alive warrant. And to make matters even worse, Doug Webb the man killer has been snooping around trying to find your trail. Shooting me in the leg of course would be an option, but what if I gave you my word that I would not pursue you for a full 48 hours after you left Grand Lake?"

Walk With Ghost reached over and patted my hand as I said to the Marshal, "I will take you at your word Marshal Robert."

Standing up, the Marshal met me half way and shook my hand. "So if you don't mind, I am going back to the front porch to finish my smoke."

After having said our goodbyes to our friends Sherol Roy and Roger Baldwin, Walk With Ghost and I made our way to the horses behind the hotel and once we were in the saddle, we pointed Spirit and Sky to the west, gave them some spur, and headed into the darkness.

CHAPTER 21

W alk With Ghost had lived as I had with almost our entire lives living on the edge of the wrong side of danger. At any moment something in our lives could cause the end of our existence. It could be severe weather, tribal hatred among the Indians, renegades both Indian and Whites, wildlife, or simply a fall from a horse. I did not have to tell her that we were in for the ride of our lives that people would be hunting us.

We rode in silence west, then southwest until we located the Colorado River. Stopping to fill the canteens and water the horses, I took the time to go through our supplies which we had purchased over three weeks ago. Howard Smith had seen fit to add the sugar that Walk With Ghost had bought just before she was shot; smiling I showed the sack to my wife and with a huge grin she gave both Spirit and Sky the treat they loved and had been missing for way too long. Both horses pawed the ground several times and snorted in anticipation. It was pleasant moments like these that I missed those that I loved.

Indicating with hand signals that we should be moving and putting more distance between Grand Lake and ourselves, we pushed the horses hard into the night following along the banks of the Colorado.

It was almost dawn when we found the tributary of the Fraser River that fed into the Colorado River. Dismounting for a breather and looking east to the top of the never summer mountains, Walk With Ghost melted backwards into my arms as we watched the day begin.

The night sky had clouded over with big fluffy clouds, and the morning sun was having some difficulty finding space enough in between to show its warming rays. Every few seconds as the clouds moved on by, we could see the sun peek through with a fiery red and orange hue. It was a sight to behold. There was a promise in each and every new dawn - a promise of new chances, a new start, and rekindled hope.

Though traveling at night, I reckoned we still had made decent time and were about 16 miles from Grand Lake. We were both tired and needed sleep and found a spot about 50 yards from the banks of the Fraser River that was surrounded by deep timber in a slight gully - a good place to be out of view from those that would be looking for us.

Unsaddling both horses and giving them a good rub down with my wooden curry comb, I hobbled them so they would not wander and let them graze in the high mountain grass. Rolling out a blanket, Walk With Ghost and I cuddled up and fell fast asleep as the "tree whispers" stirred the song of the evergreens and aspens.

The sun was at its midmorning mark in the sky when we woke up from a good solid sleep. I listened to the sounds of the day and watched the horses for a couple of minutes to see if anything was off and out of kilter with our world and sensing all was well, I gave Walk With Ghost a silent nod as we stood to ready the horses once again for the trail.

Standing at the spot where the Fraser River joined the Colorado River, I looked north and could see Berthoud Pass towering in the distance with its snowcapped peak.

Knowing the next 15 or 16 miles, crossing the Middle Park Basin that Walk With Ghost and I would be at our most vulnerable on the trip to our Redemption Valley because the terrain was the most level with the timber too far away to use as cover.

As I looked north and upstream following the Fraser River with my Italian binoculars for any sign of movement, Walk With Ghost produced a sack of roasted turkey sandwiches made with Dutch oven bread that Sherol Roy had given her just before we mounted our horses.

From my vantage point, I could see for a long distance and the snow had all but disappeared in the Fraser Valley from the long winter, and spring was now in full swing. The distant snow white clouds in the sky above moved slowly as they made their way east to west and the sun was bright and the warmth felt good on my face. The grass in the low meadows had already grown a good foot tall and moved like an ocean wave with each gust of wind. Watching the grass sway with each breeze and the sound of nearby fish jumping to catch a wayward fly in the river were pleasing to my senses on this spring day.

As peaceful as the Fraser Valley and the river that stretched out in front of us were, I knew that the many ravines and rifts of the landscape could hide a whole regiment of troopers and more easily a lone bounty hunter. Passive as it seemed, the trail north had to be treated as hostile territory.

Finishing our sandwiches, we gave our horses their head and loose reins and moved out heading north.

Moving slowly and in no hurry, I stopped every couple of hundred yards to survey the trail in front of us and also the trail behind us for movement. Once satisfied we were all alone on the Middle Park basin floor, we would continue north.

My senses were on high alert and we were always cautious as we rode along the Fraser River upstream in silence as I tried to remember what I knew about the history of this valley. After the famous Jim Bridger founded what was now called Berthoud Pass, a pioneer settler named Reuben Frazer made this valley his home and was trying to raise cattle in the Middle Park mountain plateau. Last I heard he was also trying to establish a post office six or seven miles south of Berthoud pass along the river. I am sure we were now crossing what ole' Rueben considered his pasture.

By mid-afternoon, my gut feeling was all abuzz and I felt it was time to stop and view the trail ahead once again through the Italian binoculars. Stopping below the next rise in a rift, I dismounted Spirit and moved cautiously to the top of the rift. Lying down in the high grass, I peered over the rift.

Walk With Ghost and I were on the west side of the Fraser River and on the east side of the river I saw one of the troops of ten U.S. Cavalry soldiers; this one once again was led by Master Sergeant Andy Cacy as they watered their horses in the cool water of the Fraser River.

Taking my eye off of the troopers, I turned and motioned silently for Walk With Ghost to dismount Sky, which she did. She gathered both Spirit's and Sky's reins and brought them close so she could pat their noses to keep them calm.

The soldiers were close enough that I would not need my binoculars to keep tabs on them as I lay in the high grass at the top of the rift. I did not want a run in with these troopers and would prefer that they just ride on by, but I took off the leather thong that held my pistol in my holster for safety while riding, then palmed my Colt and added one shell into the empty chamber under the hammer which was kept purposely empty also for safety. Fully loaded, I slid the Colt back into my holster.

Master Sergeant Cacy, after watering his horse and while waiting for the others to finish watering their mounts, used his military issued binoculars and started to scan the horizon in all directions. He looked directly at me not more than 50 yards away, but I could tell by the way he was holding the binoculars he was looking way beyond me and not thinking to look close.

The slight breeze was not in our favor as it was blowing north to south in the direction of the soldiers and that is why Spirit and Sky had not sensed the Cavalry horses. It was obvious the soldiers' horses were not accustomed to the wilderness trail or they would have been showing an alarm since they should be able to smell Spirit and Sky. Watching the Cavalry horses and their movements told me they were so accustomed to other horses being near them, they thought it was a natural occurrence.

Looking back to see Walk With Ghost's position, I realized she and the horses were in a low sway in the landscape and if we lay down the horses on their sides that we would probably be out of sight of the soldiers as they passed on the other side of the not very wide river.

The breeze came to a standstill and when it stopped, I could hear the soldiers talking even though I could not understand their words. We were too close for comfort.

As the soldiers were finishing watering their horses and getting themselves remounted, I slid down from the crest of the rift and made my way back to Walk With Ghost. In silence and with hand gestures, I told her what we needed to do and that was to lay both horses down and keep them quiet.

I pulled Walk With Ghost's Winchester from its scabbard and handed it to her in case she would need it. I nodded my head to tell her to take Sky down to the ground and to keep her calm by rubbing her nose and forehead.

After Walk With Ghost and Sky made it quietly to the ground, I also pulled my Winchester and without jacking a shell into the firing chamber for fear of it making too much noise, I then also pulled Spirit to the ground and lay facing the river and the soldiers while patting her snout and forehead to keep her calm.

Listening to the sounds of the river, I could also hear Master Sergeant Cacy say loudly, "Let's move out."

As the soldiers moved north on the other side of the river and closed the distance between us, I could now hear the sounds of their horses snorting and the soldiers' legs as they rubbed along the flanks of the Cavalry horses. They could be no more than fifteen yards away at this point.

Palming my Colt, I laid my arm and my pistol across Spirit's neck and pointed it in the direction of the soldiers.

Then came the sound I did not want to hear and that was the sound of a lone horse moving not north anymore, but east across the river in our direction.

CHAPTER 22

E asing back the hammer on my Colt soundlessly, I waited. I could see Walk With Ghost out of the corner of my eye as she brought her Winchester about and laid it across the neck of her mare Sky pointing in the direction of the sounds being made by the lone horseman as she lay in the high mountain grass.

The horse and the rider still were not visible yet, but close enough for me to hear the horse pawing the ground with its hoof just on the other side of the rift. The rider moved another couple of feet forward and now looking upward to the top of the rift, I could now see the horse's head and neck and a campaign hat of the Colorado 3rd Calvary as it rode on top of the head of Master Sergeant Andy Cacy.

The Master Sergeant had his military binoculars up to his eyes and was scanning the far tree line about a half mile to the east not realizing that what he was searching for was less than five yards away if he only looked down.

After what seemed an eternity but probably was less than a minute, the Master Sergeant lowered his binoculars and reined his mare back toward the Fraser River and his troop of soldiers. Andy Cacy would never know he was just a second or two away from dying in the tall grass of the Middle Park basin.

Several minutes later I could hear his horse cross back over the Fraser River to rejoin his troop as they headed north. With hand signals I told Walk With Ghost to remain where she was for now.

Waiting what I felt was 45 minutes, I crawled back to the top of the rift and looked north and could see the backs and hind quarters of the soldiers and horses as they kept moving north.

Waiting until they dropped down below a rise in the landscape and could no longer be seen is when I gave the okay sign for Walk With Ghost to let Sky and Spirit stand up.

Both horses were more than ready to stand; it is tough on large animals such as horses to lie on their sides for an extended period of time because the sheer weight of the animal can cause blood flow problems and fluid buildup,

Once Spirit and Sky were standing, we took the time to give them both a good rub down to get their blood flowing normally. After talking quietly to both and telling them how proud we were that they did not give our position away, we fed them a generous treat of sugar which they both enjoyed.

With only about an hour left of daylight, we continued south not wanting to make camp out in the open of the Middle Park basin. I would feel better once we made the tree line just at the base of Berthoud Pass.

A couple of hours after the sun had dropped down below the western horizon, we made the base of Berthoud Pass and in the shadows of a large stand of evergreens and finally feeling we were out of sight from any searching eyes in the Frazer Valley, we made camp.

After unsaddling and seeing to the horses, I spread out our bedroll for the night.

As soon as the sun had dropped out of sight, the air had grown cold and we could see our breath; I felt for Walk With Ghost's sake we needed to start a fire for some warmth. After I told her we were not going to have a cold camp, a smile spread across her face as she happily gathered stones for a campfire as I gathered some kindling and down firewood.

Once we had a fire to provide some heat, Walk With Ghost and I sat down on our bedroll and flannel blankets and leaned up against a log that I had pulled from the forest for this reason. As we finished up the last of the roasted turkey sandwiches that Sherol Roy had provided, we watched the fire in silence.

Walk With Ghost and I rarely talked in the wild for in silence there is safety. Human voices were an unnatural sound in the wilderness and the sound of voices carry for long distances in the woods and the timber. We knew each other so well and had spent the majority of our lives together, so we could communicate with gestures and looks when needed. With so many searching for us, now was the time it was needed.

We did not speak of the close call today with the soldiers of the Colorado 3rd, because what was done - was done. There was no need to rehash the past when each step and each mile on our trip to our forever home in our Redemption Valley brought the new possibility of danger and possible death.

With my right arm around my wife as she burrowed into my chest, I watched the dying orange and yellow embers as they floated and danced above on the rising heat waves of the fire. Smelling the musky smoke and the scent of pine in the air reminded of years gone by. The night and the darkness were silent except for the occasional whispering hiss and the sizzling cracks and pops of our fire.

Right now caught up in this moment with the woman I love in my arms, I felt I was the most blessed man in the Rocky Mountain frontier.

Walk With Ghost stirred against me, and I realized she had fallen to sleep. Pulling the blanket up tighter and tucking us both in, I soon joined her as I closed my eyes.

Waking before Walk With Ghost as the morning sun just started to break the top of the evergreen tree line to the east, I started to think about the day's task as we traverse Berthoud Pass.

Having traveled over the pass several times in my life, I realized that although not as dangerous as trying to go over it in the early winter, it was still dangerous in early spring. Berthoud Pass topped out about 1500 feet above the timberline, and the weather could change and become deadly in just a matter of minutes. On top of the world you were at the most vulnerable against anything that the Lord seemed fit to throw your way from an early spring avalanche, white out blizzards, wind so treacherous that it can take a muscular horse right off its feet, or a lightning strike from being at such lofty altitudes. Crossing the "Great Divide" at any time of year can be a daunting adventure on any of the Rocky Mountain high passes. You need to trust your gut instinct and have your mind right, and you need to be willing to back off if things don't feel right. At the same time, you have to push through your doubts and fears.

From the north side of Berthoud to the south side, it is about 18 miles and an almost impossible task on this rugged terrain to complete in one day. My plan was on this day to camp just below timberline to still have the protection of the evergreens from the wind. Then start again on the following day to get over the top where the trees never grow and back down in the timber on the south side so that we would never get caught on top at night.

After Walk With Ghost woke up, we ate a cold breakfast of elk jerky and hard biscuits with cold river water. After saddling and packing Spirit and Sky, we were ready to start the uphill climb.

Since the air was chilled and only would get colder the higher we climbed, I was wearing my winter duster and fox fur hat. Walk With Ghost was wearing deerskin pants and a long sleeve shirt with a long flannel poncho and on her head she wore an almost identical fox fur cap.

By midafternoon we had reached a point about 500 feet below timberline that had good protection from the wind in a thick stand of evergreen trees to make camp.

Roasted rabbit and beans were what was for supper after having shot three Jackrabbits during our climb today. As Walk With Ghost gathered wood and kindling for a cook fire, I took care of the horses by rubbing them down and feeding them some grain knowing they would need the extra energy for tomorrow. Looking above and up the trail, I watched the wind and the drifting snow play havoc above timberline before the sun finally set below the western horizon. The swirling snow that was above and in front of us told me that the next coming day would not be a pleasant one as we would attempt our final ascent to the crest of Berthoud Pass.

CHAPTER 23

After a breakfast of roasted rabbit, beans and campfire tortillas, I prepared the horses as Walk With Ghost extinguished the fire, and once done we were mounted and ready to push forward and upward.

The day like my mood was turning unpleasant, for the sun had not made an appearance at dawn and the sky was cloudy with more than enough wind to make the snow that never melts above timberline start to drift.

As we broke timberline - the line between protection from the trees and no protection from the wind at all - I stopped for a minute to look at the barren world before us on top of Berthoud Pass and what I saw was cold and uninviting swirling snow.

Walk With Ghost, feeling my displeasure of the moment, walked Sky her mare past Spirit and me and said with a smile as she passed, "Snowflakes are just kisses from the Great Spirit - nothing more."

Smiling as she took the lead, because once again, I was reminded of how perfect my wife was. She viewed the world not full of danger, but a world full of reminders why it was wonderful to be alive.

We followed a trail on the east side where the wind had kept the snow to only a foot deep instead of some places where it could be 30 feet deep even at this time of year. There was never any summer and just a tad bit of spring here above timberline and on top of the world.

The wind and the drifting snow as bad as it was, was not bad enough that I could not keep Walk With Ghost, who was just a few yards ahead of me, within my sight. We rode in total silence, for we knew that a voice with just the right pitch could start an avalanche.

Living in the Rocky Mountains, I have seen more avalanches than I care to admit since they are not a rare thing in the midst of winter and early spring. I have heard tales from those who walked these mountains of old before me that if the Lord had seen fit to drop an avalanche on your head, that the only way to survive was to swim your way out of it like you were in a river. I asked these mountain men who would tell me this if they had survived such an ordeal. None of them had actually ever been caught up in an avalanche. To this day I have never met a man or woman who had survived an avalanche, which is all I needed to know about the deadly snow slip. Having my own thoughts about being buried in one, I could only imagine that once the roll was over and if you had survived the initial onslaught, and if by chance you could move your arms, you would not have a clue of which way was up or which way was down and that it was a 50 percent chance of digging in the wrong direction and to your own demise.

Just as the thought of the dangers of an avalanche crossed my mind, I could hear the rumblings and the groan of the mountain from all around us as an avalanche began moving. Not sure if it was ahead of us or behind us or worse yet above us, I moved forward quickly to grab Walk With Ghost's hand. She turned to me with not a look of fear, but of concern as we waited for our fate.

As quickly as the rumblings had started, they stopped. Walk With Ghost's grip tightened as the now eerie silence engulfed us as if all sound had been sucked into the snow. The avalanche that had happened on the mountain was nowhere near us, and we exhaled the breath that we had taken and held at the moment of not knowing. The snow slip had happened far enough away from us that we saw nothing of its aftermath, which I can assure you was just fine with me.

Squeezing Walk With Ghost's hand and smiling to reassure her that we were in fact still alive and kicking, I leaned into her so I could whisper, "Snowflakes are kisses - my ass."

A smile spread across her face, and I could tell she was having a difficult time trying to keep her laughter from coming forth. Smiling myself, I indicated with a nod that we should keep moving and I took point this time.

Just minutes after the sounds of the avalanche had ceased, so did the wind. It didn't just die down but stopped as if someone shut a door on it and the ground blizzard we were experiencing suddenly disappeared, opening up a view to us looking south that took our breaths away. I felt sorry for those that never stood on top of the world such as we were doing and have never experienced the Lord's handiwork from such lofty heights. There would be no way that I could count the miles on how far Walk With Ghost and I could see as we took in the grandeur of it all.

What we had not seen above because of the ground blizzard caused by the wind was that the sky was clear as far as we could see and the mid afternoon sun was warming the earth. Bending over and meeting Walk With Ghost half way, I kissed her full on the lips. This woman, this princess of the Ute nation, not only kissed my lips, but she also kissed my soul each and every time we touched lips. This would have been the perfect moment except for the knowledge that there were those that were trailing us and meant to do us harm. Our eyes held each other's as we broke our embrace.

Letting the reins loosen, we gave Spirit and Sky their heads as we moved forward and downward as we left "The Great Divide" and the top of the world behind.

Our timing turned out to be perfect in that we had made the shelter of the evergreens below timberline about an hour before sunset and were able to set up a decent camp out of the snow and wind.

Our camp also had a nice bubbling brook of melting snow for Spirit and Sky to drink from. After filling our canteens with the cold mountain water, I started to take care of the horses as Walk With Ghost gathered what was needed for us to have a warming fire tonight.

After using the curry comb and rubbing down the horses, I fed them a little sugar for a treat. I left both horses loose and not hobbled so they could feast on the sparse new high mountain grass that was starting to take hold. Both Spirit and Sky seemed to enjoy the new grass. Frying up some beans to go with the last of our rabbit, I also pulled out for a tasty dessert a can of peaches we had bought in Grand Lake the day the trooper shot Walk With Ghost.

After watching the sun dip out of sight to the west, Walk With Ghost and I cuddled and spoke of our new home in Redemption Valley. Although we had never actually ever lived in the valley, we had talked about it so much that it did feel like home to us. In our hearts and minds it was home and always will be.

Walk With Ghost fell asleep with a smile on her face thinking good thoughts of our hidden valley. Watching her sleep was and will always be one of my favorite pastimes.

Tonight as I watched her sleep, I remembered a conversation I had with her years ago about angels. Now the Ute believe in "The Great Spirit," and there is no mention of angels, or what Christians would call angels. The Utes believed in spirits and those that may or may not still walk the earth, but they really had no concept of what an angel was, which in the case of Walk With Ghost always baffled me, because she was the angel that was sent to save me from myself. The way I saw it was my wife had lived with the Utes, but was an angel sent to walk among them. Her wings were hidden of course, but there was no disguising the peace and hope she brought with her. All that know her - Indian and White alike - were better off having known her than they were before. She calmed the waters and my soul; she laid to rest the evil and the beast that use to be me. Walk With Ghost meant more to me than life itself.

That is why I needed to protect her from those that hated her simply because she was an Indian. Tucking her in better underneath the flannel blanket, I started to think of those that were hunting us. In reality they were only hunting me, but without me who would protect the one I loved? No one was the answer! I needed to stay alive, not for me - my fate in the hereafter had already been cast down from the heavens above - but for her...my love...my angel.

CHAPTER 24

Waking before the sun broke the eastern horizon, I stirred the ashes into a small flame and added some kindling and then some wood when the flames got big enough.

The air was chilly this morning and I noticed some of the aspen buds had turned into leaves during the night as life renewed itself here on the south side of Berthoud Pass.

I gave the "come to" whistle to call both horses as Walk With Ghost made us a quick breakfast of fried beans and campfire tortillas. As I brushed down the horses, I thought about what was next on the trail for us. Once we finally reached the bottom of the pass, we would follow Clear Creek southwest heading toward the silver camps of Georgetown and Silver Plume.

From where we are camped this morning, I reckoned it was 19 or 20 miles to Georgetown and the north side of Guanella Pass, which was our next crossing over the "Great Divide" as we made our way to Redemption Valley.

After reaching the bottom of the pass, I saw Clear Creek in the distance about 400 yards and right next to the river were two men watering their horses. Taking out my Italian binoculars to study the men and once having them in focus, I realized they were studying me with their binoculars.

With no need to hide since Walk With Ghost and I had already been spotted, I studied the two men for a spell. And it was not long before I realized who these two men were. And by their reaction, they realized who I was by how much they were pointing and jabbering to one another. No use trying to outrun them or hide from them at this point. Hell, I was never much on running and hiding anyway. Nodding toward Walk With Ghost, we both pulled our Winchesters from their saddle scabbards and then using the lever action of the rifle jacked a 44 shell into the firing chamber.

Palming my Colt pistol, I then spun the barrel to the empty slot and added a 44 cartridge to bring me to a full load of 6. If I was to go up against the likes of Dane and Craig Snyder, then I needed to be loaded for bear and bring Hell along with me for the showdown.

Dane and Craig Snyder were brothers born out of hatred for all northerners and had fought for the losing side in the War Between the States. Some say they were murderers, bank robbers and outlaws of the worst sort, but somehow to the best of my knowledge they always stayed on the right side of the law. Just like Doug Webb, the two brothers came out of the war and became man hunters for the bounty.

And just like Doug Webb, they were the worst of the worst of humanity. Killed those they hunted not just for the money, but because they liked to kill and bounty hunting gave them the lawful means to do so. I also realized, given my past and the things that I had done, that at the end of this life I would be judged in the hereafter just as harshly as these men would be. One thing I knew that they didn't know was now I was the better man, for I had made peace with who I had been and who I was now.

A couple of years ago in the new town of Castle Rock, Colorado I had bested these two chumps in some stud poker, and it almost turned into a shooting match except I had quickly pinned Craig Snyder's hand to the poker table with my bowie knife as I held off his brother, pointing my Colt at his noggin - a wound and a slight to their manhood I am sure they have never forgotten.

Still studying them as they sat on their horses trying to figure out what to do, I knew this was not a chance meeting. They probably heard on the telegraph wire and were looking to make the $2000 bounty on me. They had come hunting me and they did not plan on taking me alive to collect. I also knew what they would do to Walk With Ghost if I should fail in defending her and myself against these men. That knowledge alone is why I had already made the decision to kill these men not only because it was self-defense, but also because my sole purpose in life was to protect my wife.

Knowing the Snyder brothers were more apt to be back shooters from ambush than fight head on, I decided to take the fight to them. My thinking was it would give me the advantage and not give them time to decipher a workable defense.

Walking Spirit up to Walk With Ghost and Sky, "Do you know who these men are?"

Walk With Ghost nodded "yes" and replied, "Bounty Hunters?"

Reaching over and taking her hand, "Yes, and the worst type of bounty hunters. They are Dane and Craig Snyder and they will not be looking to take me alive. I had a run-in with these two down in Castle Rock that did not end on friendly terms. They want me dead and that means I will have to kill both of them today. I am not going to give them a chance to think about how they will get me; I am going to take the battle to them fast and hard and bring hell and the devil with me. Do you understand?"

With a look of concern - not for herself but for me - she said, "Yes I do!"

I looked over my shoulders at the brothers and they still were in the same spot trying to figure out what to do. Looking back at Walk With Ghost, "They are about 400 yards away and I am going to sprint Spirit right at them and when I am about 200 yards away from them, I need you to move toward them until you are about 100 yards away, which will bring you close enough to finish them off with your Winchester if I fall in battle. No mercy and no quarter given, these men mean to do us both harm. If I fail in killing them, then you must finish it."

Not giving Walk With Ghost a chance to respond, I leaned over and kissed her full on the lips and then spun Spirit in the direction of the Snyder brothers and gave her some spur.

Spirit was at a full gallop when her stride smoothed out enough to let loose of the reins, and I raised my Winchester to my shoulder for a somewhat stable platform to shoot from.

Dane and Craig Snyder, as were their horses, were taken by complete surprise as I hoped they would be with my all out frontal attack. Once they started to respond, I had already closed the gap considerably. Once they were able to finally pull their rifles from their scabbards, I was within 150 yards and closing fast. Their horses were startled at Spirit and me closing so fast as were the two bounty hunters who were fumbling as they tried to pull and use their Winchesters. The horses began to buck which threw off any stable area the Snyder brothers had to shoot from.

Zeroing in on the one on the right who happened to be Dane, I fired once and missed and then fired again, and the 44 slug found a home as he dropped his rifle, grabbed his chest, and went head over butt backwards into the flowing water of Clear Creek as his horse jumped and pitched a fit.

Having now closed the distance to within 80 yards, I watched Craig fire three times as I pushed hard forward. The first two weren't even close, but I felt the heat of the third as it seared and took some meat out of my right cheek. Another half inch more and it would have been "turn out the lights" for Matt Lee.

Firing twice at Craig and missing both times now at 30 yards, I zeroed in and took my time. Spirit was forced to jump a log that was hidden in the tall grass which caused me not only to miss, but also to lose my grip on the Winchester as it tumbled out of my hand hitting the ground behind me.

At the exact moment I dropped my Winchester, Craig Snyder the bounty hunter had gotten his horse under control and stable as he lined up for a killing shot as I reached for my pistol which was still in my holster.

I hoped his shot would miss because I knew full well that I was not going to be able to pull my Colt and aim with any accuracy before he fired. Just as that thought crossed my mind, I heard the report of a rifle being fired behind me and I watched as Craig grabbed his chest just below his neck line and took a hard tumble backwards out of the saddle into the high grass lining Clear Creek's bank.

Less than a minute later, Spirit and I made it to where the Snyder brothers were down and pulling back on the reins, I finally brought a halt to Spirit's headlong gallop. As Spirit nervously pranced after such a sweat-drenched ride, I looked back at Walk With Ghost as she was just now putting away her Winchester after shooting Craig Snyder out of the saddle. I shook my head in amazement as I realized this woman that I had chosen to be my wife had saved my bacon.

CHAPTER 25

With my Colt in my hand, I reined Spirit toward Dane Snyder as he lay in the water of Clear Creek, and it was obvious by the position of his arms and legs he was sure enough dead to this world.

Moving more cautiously toward the high grass where Craig Snyder had been pitched after Walk With Ghost had shot him out of the saddle, I could hear a considerable amount of cussing.

Dismounting Spirit, I spoke to the high grass since I could not see Craig, "Are you still armed Craig? If so pitch any weapon out here where I can see it."

With anger and in pain, "Go to hell Matt Lee! I dropped my rifle and Colt when that damn squaw of yours shot me. That's not fair having your woman back shoot me like that."

I walked over so I could see Craig as he lay in the grass. As I squatted and pulled a wheatgrass to chew on, pondering what to do next with the wounded bounty hunter, "As I recall she was facing you with no back shooting involved."

Holding his right hand to his chest as the blood oozed out of his chest wound, Craig grimaced as he spoke again, "Not right letting your woman shoot me like that, just not right - damn it. I think she killed me! This hurts like hell and the blood is not going to stop flowing, I am afraid."

Looking at Craig as he was bleeding out in front of me, I could only agree with his dire prediction of his situation. His face had already gone pale from blood loss as his life slowly seeped out of his chest. "I reckon you are right, doesn't look good from here. You got to admit that was one hell of a shot."

Craig in all his pain still gave a slight chuckle, "Damn straight it was a good shot! You got one hell of a squaw there Matt Lee. What about Dane? I don't hear much yapping coming from his direction."

Watching the bounty hunter as his life started to fade and still squatting and chewing on the wheat grass I replied, "Deader than hell and lying in the creek as fish food."

Still in a death grimace and through gritted teeth, "Seems sort of fitting for my brother really; he was always sour on life and the only time I think he was happy was when he was fishing."

Walk With Ghost rode Sky up and dismounted and squatted next to me with her hand on my shoulder as I spoke to the dying bounty hunter, "Short of trying to save your life or patching you up, is there anything I could do for you Craig?"

Craig Snyder was staring at Walk With Ghost, but not in anger as he spoke, "You are a lucky man Matt Lee; not only can she shoot, but she is a looker. If you got a smoke I would be much obliged."

Nodding toward Walk With Ghost indicating she should get my corncob pipe and tobacco, "Don't have any papers, just a corncob pipe. Would that do for your last smoke, Craig?"

Craig gasping some for breath, "Would do indeed and that would be right nice of you Matt Lee. You know this was not personal, just business. $2000 is a lot of money!"

After packing the end of the corncob pipe and lighting it, I took a deep draw to get a good ember glowing and handed it to the dying bounty hunter. "I know Craig, you and your brother just bucked the wrong bronco this time."

Craig Snyder reached painfully out with his bloody right hand for the pipe and took in a deep lungful of smoke and with a smile on his face spoke the last words he would ever speak in this world, "That is mighty fine tobacco you got there Matt Lee."

After Craig Snyder, bounty hunter, finally took his last breath, I took my corncob pipe and finished off the bowl of burning tobacco and once again pondered what I now should do with the bodies of two very dead bounty hunters.

What troubled me most was not only did I have the U.S. Cavalry, Marshal Eric Robert, and Doug Webb behind me, but also it would seem the Lord through the use of the telegraph wire has seen fit to put those that mean us harm in front of us as we made our way to home to our hidden Redemption Valley. I took no pleasure in the fact that two men died today, but it was them or us; it was as simple as that...black and white with no gray area.

Walk With Ghost had retrieved my Winchester which I had dropped in my all out frontal attack of the Snyder brothers and the stock had cracked, rendering the rifle useless. I had already decided to take the bounty hunters' Winchesters and Colts and any 44 ammo they may have been carrying along with any edible food and money they may have had - not like they had any need for it now.

Walk With Ghost and I unsaddled both of the dead men's horses and then gave them a rub down with our curry comb. After feeding the mares some grain that the bounty hunters had and some sugar from our supplies, we set them free and tried shooing them away. They didn't go far and just started to graze in the tall mountain grass.

Leaving the saddles on the bank of Clear Creek in plain sight for those that may need them more than us, I left the bodies of the Snyder brothers where they had fallen. Offering up my corncob pipe to the dying Craig Snyder was just as far as my generosity extended to those that meant to kill me for money. As far as I was concerned, the critters needed to eat also.

We must have come along the bounty hunters after they had been fishing in cool mountain waters of Clear Creek because they had four freshly gutted rainbow trout, and along with some wild onions that Walk With Ghost had found, we made a campfire and fried up the trout and onions for our midday meal.

After finishing off the tasty trout that had been supplied by the dead bounty hunters, we mounted Spirit and Sky and turned our horses southwest to follow Clear Creek toward Georgetown and Guanella Pass.

Looking back at the body of Dane Snyder one last time, I saw a couple of large crows land on his body and they started to peck at the soft flesh of his neck and eyes.

Life was tough on the Rocky Mountain frontier. One day you are top of the food chain; the next day you become the bottom of the food chain, and it has always been that way. The only difference between man and the critters that lived in these high mountains is that most of the time men could be crueler than the animals in how they treated their own. I was no different than those that had perished today in that regard.

An hour before we found our campsite for the night about two miles northeast of Georgetown, we had ridden the horses in the river bed, leaving no tracks except those for the most experienced tracker to follow. We moved our horses out of Clear Creek and into the timber where we would be somewhat hidden, but with some protection from the wind. From my vantage point I could see the whole south side of Berthoud Pass and while eating a cold supper of elk jerky, I studied the mountain with my binoculars.

Twenty minutes or so before sunset I saw the glint of the sun off probably the glass of another set of binoculars or some polished metal. Focusing on and adjusting my binoculars on the mountainside, I was not surprised by what I saw - troopers numbering ten from the Colorado 3rd were slowly making their way down the steep terrain off Berthoud Pass. Looking above them and slightly to the west, I saw a lone man on horseback and I recognized the horse even from this great distance. Doug Webb and his Appaloosa mare Cimarron were headed in our direction. Studying the mountain until the sun dipped so far out of sight I could no longer see, I did not see Marshal Eric Robert, but knew in my heart he was on our trail as well. I respected a man who took his oath and job seriously. Knowing our pursuers were more than a day away, I decided not to worry Walk With Ghost with what I saw just before sunset.

Walk With Ghost had already fallen asleep and I watched her for a spell. I always felt closer to her at moments like these when she did not know I was watching her. In her sleep, she was completely defenseless, soft, and childlike. Slowly lying down and cuddling up with her so I would not wake her, I thought about how our hard exteriors slowly melted away as soon as the sandman brought sleep. I could not for the life of me think of anything more beautiful as sleeping next to the one I loved. It was moments like these that I wished I was a painter or even an author of books and words so I could capture it forever.

Pondering the fact that possible death was indeed behind us and in front of us, I did not let that fact fester in this moment of peace with my wife. As I held her hair and slightly rubbed it in between my finger and thumb, I too fell asleep.

CHAPTER 26

Waking before dawn, I wanted to be well past the mining camp of Georgetown before most folks were up and moving. Walk With Ghost and I ate a cold breakfast of hard biscuits and elk jerky. After seeing to the horses and saddling them, we moved out to the southwest once again.

We rode on the west side of Clear Creek trying to keep to the shadows as we passed the mining camp of Georgetown. I couldn't see from where we were, but I knew the mining camp of Silver Plume was up the mountain and to the west about one mile. The smell of wood smoke was heavy in the air as the people of the mining camp woke and started their daily routines of making coffee and their breakfast. Approaching Guanella Pass, which was on the very southwest side of Georgetown, we found a shallow ford to cross Clear Creek from west to east. Minutes after leaving the cold waters of the river, we started our upward climb up the north side of Guanella.

Thinking about what I knew about Guanella Pass and the trail ahead, I knew it was not a pass one wanted to try during the winter because it would sure enough be the death of you. Even in the spring it could be treacherous and deadly at 1500 feet above timberline. The snow at the top never melted at those lofty elevations and just like Berthoud Pass, there was the possibility of white outs if the wind got to blowing across the bald top with no trees to slow the drifting snow.

From where Walk With Ghost and I were now, it would be 25 miles to the north fork of the South Platte river. Sky and Spirit were feeling good in this clear and beautiful spring day with only a few puffy white clouds to keep us company, and they were making excellent time, not seeming to tire at the ever-increasing altitude.

By midmorning after passing several large ponds that I could not recall their name, we could see the top of Sugarloaf Peak directly to the east of us.

As we rode south in silence through the aspens and evergreens, I started to ponder on those behind us. The more I thought about it, I decided the Colorado 3rd was the least of my worries. They were young and inexperienced in tracking and I am sure I lost them when we crossed Clear Creek not soon after our encounter with the Snyder brothers. I had no such illusions about the bounty hunter Doug Webb or the Territorial Marshal Eric Robert. Both men were experienced man hunters even though they did not have any idea where I was headed.

My pondering on this subject made me sure about one thing and that was the bounty hunter Webb. The Marshal, I was sure in time due to the pressing matters of his job, would probably give up the search for me if I was not found quickly. Doug Webb's only job, on the other hand, was me and his only payday was bringing me in dead; he was not about to give up the hunt. He out of all the others was the one who might stumble upon our Redemption Valley. There might come a point in time that we could not run any longer and I would have to turn and fight the man. There had already been way too much death in my life caused by me. I would prefer never again spilling the blood of another man. Then again, my sole purpose for living now was to protect my lady love Walk With Ghost. If I had to kill to do that, then there would not be any hesitation or second thought on the matter. Turning and fighting? I will still have to roll it around in my mind for a spell.

Coming out of a stand of aspens that had been quaking to the tune of the "tree whispers," we came across a couple of mountain goats high up on the mountainside above the tree line and to our west. The only time I had ever seen these magnificent animals was on this pass. Taking a few minutes, Walk With Ghost and I watched as they sprinted and hoofed over boulders that no man could climb with what seemed little or no effort on their part. These goats I had been told could survive down to 50 below zero with their snow white, wooly double coats. Male and female, both had beards, short tails, and long black horns. You could tell that spring was in full swing even up high in the Rocky Mountain frontier, and these mountain goats had already started to molt and shed the extra winter wool. The male billy goats, even though they had seen us watching them, took little interest in the likes of us since they knew that we were no threat to them upon their lofty steep mountainside.

We decided, since the day was such a glorious day with no sign of bad weather in the offering, to push on and over the top of Guanella. So at midday we ate a cold meal in our saddles of elk jerky as we kept moving. I had another reason for not stopping, but was not going to tell Walk With Ghost just yet. She did not know I had seen the troopers of the Colorado 3rd and Doug Webb and that they all had been moving in our direction yesterday. I wanted to keep putting time and miles in between us and those that wanted my head.

By mid-afternoon both horses, still showing no sign of the high altitude causing them discomfort, were still able to make great progress as we breached the top of the pass. Once again Walk With Ghost and I sat on top of the world knowing some men and women would never have the courage to ride these lordly heights in the thin air and take a gander at the world below. Even though we were now sitting 1500 feet above where trees never grow and summer never melts the snow, we could see even the highest mountains to our east of Mount Bierstadt and Mount Evans both which topped out at over 4000 feet above timberline.

To our west we could see the very beginning of Duck Creek that was flowing at a high rate with the snow starting to melt as it flowed on to the south into Duck Lake which would be our next camp before dark.

We followed Duck Creek as it flowed downward and southward. The horses had plenty of water and spring grass for the extra strength it took to walk the high trails and passes in the Rocky Mountains. It was just an hour before sundown that we made it to the banks of Duck Lake that was lined with evergreens and a few aspens. It was evident by the number of geese and ducks that lined the banks and were floating in the water how Duck Lake got the name.

Walk With Ghost was able to bring down a goose with a well thrown rock for our supper this evening. Living amongst the Utes, I learned that the women were deadly hunters when it came to rock throwing for food, and I had seen many of the young bucks of the Ute Nation take a few well-placed rocks when their women were mad at them. As an outsider, one learned not to ask about the large goose egg seeping blood when one that had taken a rock from his wife to the noggin. The young men of the Ute tribes always laughed at those that had been punished in such a manner until it happened to them. Luckily, Walk With Ghost in 30 some years had not felt the need to punish me by thumping me with a rock. I learned of her deadly aim early on and felt the need to stay on her good side.

Walk With Ghost gathered wood for a cooking fire as I tended to Spirit and Sky. As soon as she got a good fire going, she started to roast the goose on a sapling with some more of the wild onions she had found on Clear Creek.

After unsaddling both horses, I gave them a good rub down and spoke gently about how proud I was of them for not faltering today in the thin air above timberline. They were truly bred for the wilderness and the mountains and this wild frontier. After feeding them both a generous portion of sugar for a much deserved treat, I went to help Walk With Ghost finish our supper.

Not having goose in quite a spell, I enjoyed the tasty retreat from venison and elk and the crispy campfire onions with a little salt tasted even better.

It was times like these with my wife that were so peaceful in nature that made life worth living. For this evening I put the thoughts of those chasing us in the back of my mind. It would not be long now that I would have to face the men that were following us; there would be no getting around that, but for tonight I would just enjoy the cool spring air, good food, and time with the woman I love.

After supper Walk With Ghost and I cuddled on our bedroll listening to the music of the mountains. "Music of the mountains" was not a phrase I would have ever thought of...Lord no, I was never that smart. It was the name of a poem that had been written by my good friend Sam Walters many years ago before he and the others were killed at La Caverna Del Oro on Marble Mountain. Thinking back on what happened so many years ago, I realized how much I missed all my dear departed friends, but I think what I missed most was Sam's music and his poetry. "Music of the Mountains" I knew by heart; I always thought it spoke directly to me. Even though Walk With Ghost had heard it many times, she never stopped me when I started to recite it. She knew I needed to speak the words to be close to those that I loved like brothers.

Holding my wife tight, I spoke to the night wind and the trees, and I spoke Sam's words -

"Music of the Mountains"
Early on in life, I heard the message, the call,
Down through the years it got stronger as I recall.
Music of the mountains was so pleasant to the ear,
Sounds of nature in the mountains so crystal clear.
The hoot of an owl, crisp wind tickling the trees,
Rain drops on a fallen log - all of this was music to me.
"Home is where your heart is," It has been said,
True enough - Rocky Mountains straight ahead.

Reaching over to wipe away a single tear that had leaked from my eye, Walk With Ghost spoke quietly, "You are a good man Matt Lee and your heart is pure. Others may not see it, but I know this to be true."

As soon as she was done talking, she pulled back our top blanket and slowly started to undress herself. Watching her as she shed her clothes, I started to undress myself.

CHAPTER 27

Waking before dawn, I stirred the ashes of our fire to expose the glowing embers to the air until I got a small flame; I added some kindling and then a couple of small logs so that we had a fire sufficient to cook with. Making campfire tortillas to go with the last remnants of the goose that Walk With Ghost killed yesterday, we had the makings of a fine breakfast this morning.

The breakfast may have been fine, but the weather was starting out a little sketchy. Dark clouds had moved in from the north during the night - ones that looked menacing and possibly full of rain or even snow at this time of year.

After I gave the "come to" whistle, both Spirit and Sky made their way to the campsite, both seeming to be a tad on edge. They were sensing the storm. Knowing full well that animals have a sixth sense when it comes to danger, I took it since both of the horses were on edge, that this approaching storm was not a typical storm.

And just to prove my point as I looked north, I saw a blackened cloud flash that could only have come from lightning within the cloud itself. Seeing lightning this early in the morning told me this was going to be a dangerous storm. It had always been my experience that thunder and lightning storms were rare in the mornings. I had not any facts on this matter other than from personal experience, but to me it seemed like a rare occurrence indeed.

Moving more quickly, I helped Walk With Ghost take care of our campsite to hide any sign that we had been here at all. Being an Indian, my wife was very good at leaving no trail in the wilderness. We did not want to make it easy on those that meant us harm.

After saddling the horses, I watched from behind as Walk With Ghost mounted Sky, and even at her age, she still moved with the agility of a young girl, which in turn reminded me of last night. With a smile spreading across my face, I gave Spirit a slight jab of my spur and we moved in the same direction as Walk With Ghost as we followed the Duck Creek south as it flowed downward to Geneva Creek.

At mid-morning the wind started to pick up which dropped the temperature enough that we had to stop and put on our rawhide slickers in anticipation of some wet weather.

At around midday we found ourselves at the point where Duck Creek dumped into the much larger Geneva Creek. Knowing we were not going to outrun any storm, we stopped to have a warm meal of beans and the last of the campfire tortillas from this morning.

As we ate our meal, I studied the clouds in the north and did not see any more flashes of lightning. Not seeing the flashes in the clouds was a good thing for now; lightning in the high mountains was even more dangerous than when you were down on the plains. Its path to you was shorter and I think more powerful. They say lightning never strikes twice in the same place, but then again it didn't have to. If you happened to be in that spot it struck the first time, more than likely you would be dead to this world. A second strike was not going to matter much one way or another. Lightning was one of those things the Lord threw at you that you could never defend against in the wilderness. It was dangerous and deadly and had a mind of its own. Not seeing any more lightning flashes was a good thing.

It started to drizzle right after we had cleaned our campsite leaving no trace. It was a wet and cold drizzle and would make for a damp and muddy trail. Not leaving tracks now was not an option; the mud was a tracker's best friend and if those that were following us were close, they would able to use it to their advantage. The rain and the mud would also slow us down some. Worse case would be one of the horses would slip and fall injuring not only itself, but also the rider. Good news was, if there was some good news, it would also slow our pursuers. Then again, the more I thought about that I knew it would not slow down Doug Webb and his Appaloosa, Cimarron. According to the stories that damn horse was indestructible, and if any horse would not be slowed by mud and slippery terrain, it would be the bounty hunter's mare.

At midafternoon the cold drizzle had gathered in strength and had become sheets of hard driven rain which was both a blessing and a serious problem. A blessing that the hard rain now would wash away any tracks left behind us, and a serious problem because now we needed to find some sort of shelter and build a fire for warmth. Both Walk With Ghost's and my rain slickers were soaked all the way through and I could see Walk With Ghost's teeth chattering when I rode up closer to check on her. The chattering told me her body temperature had dropped some and she needed to get warm quickly. The Utes called it the cold death and after your body heat started to leave your body and your flesh became colder than the air, you could expect confusion, apathy, and slurred speech. The only thing the person so affected wanted to do was lie down and sleep. Falling asleep like this could cause you to die.

Looking at the mountainside and the tree line along the side of Geneva Creek, I looked for any type of shelter from the cold rain. A fire to warm our bodies was not an option at this point; it was the only thing that would keep us alive.

Not far in the distance I spotted what we needed, and riding up and grabbing Walk With Ghost's arm, I pointed toward a large granite overhang protruding out from the mountain itself on the east side of Geneva Creek. It was cut into the rock so that it blocked the driving rain and wind from the north. It also had two walls of stone on the north and east side. It was not high enough for the horses to get under, but it would be perfect for Walk With Ghost and myself. It would get us out of the rain, but also the two granite sides would reflect heat when we got a fire started.

As soon as Walk With Ghost had her feet on the ground, she went around gathering wood as I stripped the saddles off of Spirit and Sky.

Since the shelter was not large enough for the horses, I turned them both loose to seek shelter from the rain. Both horses seemed confused and huddled close until the Lord and the heavens changed their minds and the sky lit up with a brilliant and blinding flash of lightning, followed closely behind by the roar of thunder as it echoed off the mountainside. Spirit and Sky were still confused, but also scared shitless as they bolted out of sight. Knowing they were better off on their own than with us, I put their safety in the back of my mind as my own teeth started to chatter from the coldness and the coming cold death that was now starting to seep deep into my body.

The boom of thunder followed so close to the lightning strike which told me the storm was sitting on top of us. Walk With Ghost had all the makings of a fire except the spark. My hands were so cold as I struggled almost hilariously trying to use the flint stone. After a few failures I was able to get a spark to grab hold of the tender, and turning towards Walk With Ghost, I could see a smile cross her face. She knew the danger the storm and the wetness had presented.

Adding more kindling and then finally larger logs, we had a nice warming fire. After stripping down out of our rain soaked clothes, we put on a new and somewhat dry set from our saddle bags and packs. After we set our soaked clothes close to the fire to dry out, we went about making some fried beans and fatback bacon from our provisions for supper tonight. I also decided it was a good night to eat one of the last two cans of peaches we had for dessert.

The granite overhead was doing nicely keeping us warm and out of the rain. It was coming down so hard that it almost seemed like a wall of water in front of us looking into the woods and the encroaching darkness.

After each lightning strike that touched the ground, the roar of the thunder was almost on top of it. We were in the middle of the storm and it didn't seem to be letting up anytime soon. Walk With Ghost jumped each time the lightning struck and the thunder boomed. I didn't want to admit it to her, but being this close to the Lord's fury was making me jumpy also. I could not help but worry about Spirit and Sky and if they had found shelter from this hellish storm.

With so much water from the downpour and the recent melting of the snow, I could hear Geneva Creek down below us as it turned into a raging river. Our granite overhang was up high enough I did not feel threatened by any flood water. Once again my thoughts went back to the horses. I said a silent prayer that they had found shelter and they would be okay.

After supper Walk With Ghost and I held each other under the blankets for warmth as we listened to the storm rage overhead and all around us. After some time we either got used to the flashes of light and the thunder rolling off the mountains or simply we became exhausted because we both fell into an uneasy sleep.

CHAPTER 28

W alk With Ghost and I both slept in spurts, but with each flash and boom, any restful sleep was not to be had. After a stressful night of constant lightning and thunder, the storm seemed to have moved on toward the east a couple of hours before dawn leaving only a slight sprinkle.

What weighed more heavily on my mind was how Spirit and Sky had weathered the storm. When they had bolted last night, their eyes were full of fear. Any horse in a frightful flight was bound to sustain some injuries in the dark with as many down trees that scattered the forest floor. Lightning and thunder were always problems when it came to any animal.

We would need daylight to search for the horses, so in the meantime, we fried up some fatback bacon and beans and made some new campfire tortillas for our breakfast.

The dampness and the night fog that had been left behind was cold, very cold. It was all the fire could do to keep the frigidness from seeping deep into our bones. Looking into the fog and what remained of the darkness, I had a sense of foreboding and I knew today was not going to be a pleasant day.

The sky started to lighten as the new dawn made its appearance in the east. The sun itself decided to stay hidden behind the remaining dark rain clouds and early morning fog. The air was chilled and wet with a slight drizzle of the last remnants of rain. The early morning murkiness loomed as far as I could see. It was a white shroud that covered the mountain with the morning sun having a difficult time penetrating the haze. Surrounding us was an eerie silence as the damp fog absorbed all sounds of the wilderness, except one and that was a "caw, caw" that somehow made it through the thickening vapor. Before I saw it, I knew it would be a crow, a midnight black crow. Once again a sense of foreboding overcame me. The wilderness and the mountain had signaled me and the signs were all there; this was not going to be a good day - not at all.

Moving toward the "caw, caw" I finally saw what I expected to see and that was a black crow sitting on a branch of an evergreen. He was watching me as I watched him. It would seem as if I was more fearful of him than he was of me on this cold and dreary morning. I had no doubt that the presence of the crow was a sign from the Lord or the Great Spirit, but I was having a difficult time trying to decipher what it could mean. As I rolled it around some and pondered on it, the crow took flight and disappeared into the fog heading south.

Looking into the dense mist, I gave the "come to" whistle, hoping the sound would pierce the wall of silence and make it to our mares Spirit and Sky.

Walk With Ghost stood by me at the edge of the granite overhang holding my hand as I continued to give the "come to" whistle every couple of minutes hoping that the horses could hone in on it.

Hearing some movement in the woods and dense fog, I grabbed the Winchester and used the lever action to jack a round into the firing chamber. My "come to" whistle was intended for our horses, but it might be leading those that meant us harm in our direction.

A shadow appeared of a lone horse as it walked cautiously in our direction. I heard the distinct snort of Spirit my mare, speaking toward the murkiness and the shadow. "This way my friend, and am I glad to see you."

Once I got a hold of Spirit's mane, I hugged her neck and gave her some loving as Walk With Ghost walked around her looking for injuries that might have occurred in her frightful flight during the storm. Seeing none that were apparent, Walk With Ghost started on her with the curry comb as I talked to Spirit trying to calm her fears from the thunderstorm. After feeding her some grain and sugar from our packs, she seemed to be calming down and thankful for finding us.

As much as we were happy that Spirit found her way home, we were worried about Sky. It was obvious that during the hellish storm that Sky and Spirit had been separated. Every couple of minutes I would walk the perimeter of our camp and give the "come to" whistle to no avail. Sky had either bolted farther than the sound of my whistle could carry or she was injured or even worse.

As the sun started to burn away the fog, I took time to walk down to Geneva Creek and look for any tracks of Sky. The storm had washed away any and all tracks that Sky may have left during her flight, and there were no new tracks other than those of Spirit this morning. I started to feel that the sighting of the crow this morning and the feeling of dread meant that Sky was no longer coming home.

Walking back toward the granite overhang and Walk With Ghost, I started to ponder how much trouble the absence of Sky meant to our survival. One horse was going to slow us down considerably and give those that were following us time to catch up. The storm last night might have gone east, but the aftereffects may get us killed.

By the time I had made it back to our camp, I decided Sky was long gone and no longer coming back. We would have to make do without her for now as we tried to get to Redemption Valley.

The tears in Walk With Ghost's eyes told me she also feared that Sky was gone for good. Without words, we worked together trying to lighten our load of provisions and what not to the bare essentials. We would have to use Spirit as a pack horse leaving one saddle behind as Walk With Ghost and I would also have to walk, which in the spring would not be such a terrible thing if we didn't have the likes of Territorial Marshal Eric Robert, the Colorado 3rd, and the bounty hunter Doug Webb trailing and hunting us.

After getting Spirit saddled and packed, I hated leaving Walk With Ghost's saddle, but having limited space now, that was the only choice. Moving out from the granite overhang, we located Geneva Creek and started our journey once again south toward Redemption Valley.

It was at midday when we found Sky, or what was left of Walk With Ghost's beloved mare. Sky's body had been caught up in the flood waters of the raging Geneva Creek last night and washed down to the south where she now was entangled in the dead wood and tree limbs that had gotten washed down in the flash flood of the night before.

Walk With Ghost ran towards her and flopped down on the now very dead horse. Walk With Ghost filled the air with sobs of grief as she hugged Sky with all the love that she could muster. Seeing my wife so distraught brought tears to my eyes as well. I was not sure how to comfort my wife, so I just let her tears roll as her grief ran its course.

As I bent down close to Walk With Ghost, it was obvious to me that Sky first had been struck by lightning before being swept down the flood waters of Geneva Creek. I had seen livestock hit by lightning many times in my life and knew that it was not a rare thing at all for that to happen. Sky had already started to bloat as her insides started to break down. It was obvious she had burns all over her withers and down her legs. She also had a burn mark that ran down the jugular groove on the side of her neck. More than likely she died a quick death as her heart and brain were stopped by the lightning strike. Knowing Sky's death was quick was not going to help Walk With Ghost much in her despair.

Sitting on the bank watching over Spirit as she drank her fill in Geneva Creek and of course Walk With Ghost as she said her final goodbyes to her horse, I knew we should be pushing on, that those that wanted my head would be close behind, but I did not have the heart not to let Walk With Ghost have this moment. Grief was a funny thing as it came in waves. It had been my experience you learned to ride the waves on top and had to learn to swim when they were at their lowest. Walk With Ghost was stronger than most and would survive this. I did not have to rush her; she would know when it was time to move on.

A couple of hours later, after the sun had broken through the clouds and started to warm the air, Walk With Ghost walked up to me and said, "Matt Lee, we need to keep moving."

Standing up I gathered my wife in my arms and held her tight, "I reckon so, my love."

CHAPTER 29

Worrying about Walk With Ghost and her state of mind after losing her horse in such a horrific manner had to be put aside. The reality of it was that we were in trouble now - huge trouble. The sense of foreboding rolled over me like a wave. The sky was now blue and all the storm clouds had moved on to wreak havoc elsewhere, but what was left behind was that we no longer had an advantage in time and miles. Those that were trailing us now had what we no longer had and that was speed, giving them the ability to catch up to us now. Losing Sky to the lightning and the storm may in the end be the demise of us.

Moving out we started south again with Walk With Ghost walking along the side of Spirit and with me walking point. Losing Sky was going to be a problem and I rolled it around in my head some as we moved forward towards Redemption Valley.

My thoughts were that I was almost sure that the Colorado 3rd would have lost our trail and hopefully no longer able to track us.

Master Sergeant Andy Cacy knew the true score of what happened back in Grand Lake and I felt he was just going through the motions of searching for me, just because he was ordered to do so. I felt his heart was really not in it by his actions after seeing me at the window of the Baldwin Hotel and not telling his 1st Lieutenant about it, and his chief concern was the safety of those under his charge. After the recent storm I did not believe the Colorado 3rd had good enough trackers to follow me; the troopers were young boys and not battle hardened. Andy Cacy knew that many of those young men would die if he and his troopers did in fact try to capture me. I had a gut feeling that Walk With Ghost and I may have seen the last of the Colorado 3rd Cavalry.

Territorial Marshal Eric Robert was a different story. Since a warrant had been issued for my arrest, the Marshal would do anything in his power to fulfill his job until told otherwise. Just the fact that he was an older Marshal spoke volumes on how dangerous he could be. You did not live to be his age in his line of work unless you were a man not to be toyed with. If he had a mission, he would be like a dog with a bone. I realized he would be an experienced tracker because his job required that. Being handy with his weapons would also be true. I would regret very much so if the Marshal tried to arrest me, because I admire and respected him. Killing him would be an option that would not be desirable, but if it came down between him and the safety of my wife, there would be no question of what I would do.

Doug Webb the bounty hunter would not give up the chase with so much money on my head. He was a killer and man hunter who enjoyed his work. I had no illusions that Doug Webb and his Appaloosa mare Cimarron would lose our trail; he had the experience and the wherewithal to keep after our trail regardless of the storm or not. His horse, according to all the stories, had twice the stamina of other horses and would not tire easily. Doug Webb was the type of foe that if he killed me, he would also abuse and have his way with Walk With Ghost. Women were not people to men like Webb; they were used for pleasure and work and then discarded. Since my wife was Indian, I was sure that Webb would see her even lower than an animal and he would not even blink before he killed her once he was done with me and her. The man would not have a moral compass to speak of and he walked the fine line on the right side of the law only because his survival required it. He was a dangerous adversary as they came, and I knew in the end that it would come down to him or me that one of us would have to die. Doug Webb or I would die at the end of this chase across the Rocky Mountain frontier; it was just a matter of timing is all.

Even though we had been slowed because of the loss of Sky, we made good time by the time the sun started to fade in the west. We found a secluded spot for our camp tonight. The sound of running water from the creek was soothing to my soul as it swiftly flowed in Geneva Creek deep back in the aspens and evergreens. As the sky turned orange to blue, we fried up some fatback bacon and four prairie chicken eggs that we found in a nest not far from our trail.

Spirit, though not hobbled, stayed close to us and the fire tonight. It was as if she wanted to be close to those who loved her after the frightful thunder and lightning storm and the loss of her friend Sky yesterday.

Walk With Ghost and I, without speaking, did the chores that needed to be done. Our predicament was weighing heavily on the both of us. If we were lucky, then both the Marshal and the bounty hunter had lost our trail and had given up on the chase and we would be home free. My gut feeling was it may have slowed them down some, but they were still in the pursuit. My gut feeling was hardly ever wrong.

Walk With Ghost seemed to sleep peacefully through the night while I, on the other hand, slept in spurts. The feeling of dread outweighed the need to sleep. My whole life's mission, since I rescued Walk With Ghost from the mountain lion, was providing for and protecting her. It felt to me that I was starting to lose that battle and that was a feeling that I was not accustomed to. I have always been confident in my ability to provide food and shelter for her here in the Rocky Mountain frontier. I also had been confident in my abilities as a warrior to protect her. Looking toward the half-moon overhead, I said a silent prayer to the Lord and the Great Spirit.

Finally, several hours before dawn I got some good sleep only to be awakened by the "caw, caw" of a crow that had settled onto an aspen tree limb above my head just before sunrise.

The ebony crow was so loud it woke Walk With Ghost and seemed to have garnered the attention of Spirit as she grazed nearby. Spirit was watching the crow as intently as I was as if we both tried to find meaning in its presence here this morning.

My gut instinct was tossing and turning as I watched the crow. Standing up, I walked slowly over to the tree that housed the bird and after reaching a point that I was so close that if I wanted to, all I needed to do was reach out and touch the crow. The crow was not skittish at all of my closeness, nor did it fear me. That alone told me this was not a normal crow; this black bird was indeed a messenger sent to warn me that danger was close at hand.

Moving swiftly, I started to pack our belongings and dismantle the camp. Walk With Ghost felt my sense of urgency as she also started to move quickly about as we prepared Spirit and ourselves to continue our travels.

Understanding the message of danger, I did take the time to clean my Winchester and my Colt and made sure the Colt was fully loaded with six and the Winchester had a round in the firing chamber.

It had occurred to me that since we had lost the advantage of staying ahead of those that wanted to do us harm when Sky had been killed, that flight was no longer an option. Turning to face and fight our adversaries was now the only option left. My thought on this matter was we had less than 24 hours to locate a possible place from which to defend ourselves.

Having made up my mind to fight actually eased the burden on me. I was always more comfortable taking the fight to the enemy. Walk With Ghost understood my mood swing and she was prepared to go to war with me. The crow made me realize that maybe I was getting old, but I was still the man the Utes had called "Ghost," feared warrior amongst the high Rockies.

After cleaning and loading my weapons and getting ourselves and Spirit ready to travel, I looked back once more at the crow. The crow cawed only once before it took flight and flew directly over my head south. The crows' job was done and its warning had been received. I let Spirit and Walk With Ghost take point and I brought up the rear. Our danger, our foes, and those that wanted my head were behind me. I needed to be sharp-eyed and on high vigilance.

CHAPTER 30

My mind knew that danger was close at hand and it
made the switch back into my "Ghost" days, which in
truth was never far from those days as I tiptoed to the
edge of crazy and not so crazy. Guerrilla warfare was the key to
victory in what we now faced. My battle with those that hunted us
would be much easier if I did not have Walk With Ghost to defend
and protect. Having my wife here now was the only reason I was
still alive and even though she made that job of the coming battle a
tougher task, I would not have it any other way. As we moved
south, I started to brood over the problem and rolled some possible
solutions around in my mind.

By mid-morning we had located the north fork of the South
Platte River, which would be the point that we would use to start
heading almost due west to Kenosha Pass. After watering Spirit in

the river and making sure our canteens were topped off, I took some time to study our back trail with the binoculars and seeing no movement other than a couple of spring doves, we pushed on.

Though our lives were in peril as we moved steadily toward Redemption Valley, it did not take away from the fact that spring time in the Rocky Mountain frontier was in full swing. The weather today was the typical Colorado territory spring type weather with the forever blue sky stretching as far as my eyes could see with what seemed to be the clarity that you only achieved being this close to heaven's skyline. There of course was a smattering of low level flat clouds here and there which broke up the view of the far horizon which only added to the beauty of the Lord's handiwork.

The air was slightly chilled as it is almost all the time this high up in the Rockies, but left me feeling strong when I took deep breaths of it. The wind was stirring just enough to make the "tree whispers" play their mountain songs as the wind and the air tickled the aspen leaves.

Overhead a couple of red-tailed hawks were performing their magnificent courtship displays. We came across a couple of black and white magpies as they carried new sticks to spruce up their old stick nests. Yes, spring time in the Rocky Mountain frontier was in full swing for all of those that understood the way of nature.

Watching life here in the Rockies as it moved all around Walk With Ghost and me, I started to wonder with the life that I had lived, the death that I had caused, and the danger now facing us, how many more springs would I live to see?

As soon as the sun was directly overhead and at its midpoint as it made its arc across the sky, we made what I would call the base of Kenosha Pass - the doorway to South Park.

Kenosha Pass topped out about 10,000 feet just below timberline and the snow during the winter always melted on top of Kenosha since it lacked the height of other passes such as Berthoud and Guanella. Kenosha was part of the spine of the Front Range along the eastern side of South Park and by my own experience, it was an easy travel pass and that once you reached the summit, you had stunning and dramatic views of the surrounding Rocky Mountains, including the nearby peaks of Mount Evans and Mount Bierstadt.

Several years ago, my friend Lucas Eldridge had to traverse Kenosha during the dead of winter to rescue his now wife Devon, who was being held prisoner by the outlaws Irish Bob O'Conner and Rick Pryce in the town of Como.

What made Kenosha Pass more important to me on this date was that I knew of a perfect spot near the top that good be easily defended with shelter from the wind and the unpredictable weather. It also had a babbling brook of fresh clean water that sprang from the mountain itself. My thought now was that I was going to use this place as a headquarters to bring the war to Doug Webb and Marshal Eric Robert, and the Colorado 3rd Cavalry if they were still on my trail.

My killer instinct that had been honed by my years of warfare against the Ute Nation was starting to kick back in. Walk With Ghost's and my future and survival depended on my abilities as the "Ghost." Those that were close behind were hazardous foes that could not be taken lightly. The skill sets that I had learned during those years of war battling the Utes were dangerous, deadly, and became the death of many that chose to go to war against me. I also realized it was over 30 years ago and the best of my youth was behind me and old age and tired muscles had replaced the young and not so tired muscles. My mind was still sharp and clear, and hopefully that would be my biggest advantage of what was coming.

At mid-afternoon Walk With Ghost and I located the spot just below timberline that I was looking for, and it was just as I remembered right down to the babbling brook. The place that I had chosen to make war from was sheltered on three sides with a granite overhang and deep dark stand of evergreen trees that was difficult to walk through let alone ride a horse through.

Once locating our new base camp, I left Walk With Ghost alone to unpack Spirit and make camp as I scouted the surrounding terrain. I put out the three jump traps I had to hopefully trap a rabbit or a wayward squirrel or two.

The front of our camp had a natural stone wall that ranged between two to three feet as it ran along the perimeter. It also had a fairly steep incline just beyond the wall which gave me the advantage of being higher than anyone attempting to attack our camp and giving me a clear view of the trail down below. During daylight hours I would have a great advantage with the Italian binoculars. I was still rolling it around in my brain pan thinking it might be the wiser choice to leave Walk With Ghost here and take the battle to my enemy. Leaving Walk With Ghost all alone was not desirable, but still may be the better option. I was still pondering on that aspect when I heard one of the small jump traps snap closed, meaning dinner was going to be some sort of meat tonight.

The snowshoe rabbit caught in the trap was a big one about four pounds and would be ample enough for both Walk With Ghost and myself.

I cleaned the rabbit on the camp side of the natural wall while I kept looking down below for any movement that would indicate that the bounty hunter, or the Marshal, or the Cavalry was still on my trail.

Walk With Ghost had already gotten a cook fire started and came and took the rabbit from me as I studied the terrain down below looking for any sign that we were being tracked and hunted.

As the sun started to fade to the west and drop below the horizon and the trees, the light also faded to the point that I could no longer look into the ever-growing shadows of the trees. Night would be the time when we would more apt to be attacked. I would from now on keep Spirit close to us to use her keen eyesight, smell, and her ability to hear better than I for hopefully any advance warning of danger. My gut instinct told me that this night probably was not the night for any encounter, but tomorrow or more likely tomorrow night was when they would catch up.

After a filling supper of roasted rabbit, fried beans, and campfire tortillas, Walk With Ghost and I cleaned our weapons and counted our ammo. I even sharpened my Bowie knife and all of our skinning knives.

We spoke of what to expect and I even told her I might take the battle to them and leave her here alone; she did not say so, but I could see it in her eyes she was not at all in favor of that option. After seeing Walk With Ghost's reaction to the notion I might leave her alone, I decided that was no longer an option. We would fight here and together, knowing full well that probably was what was going to happen anyway.

We kept the fire going since there was plenty of downed firewood lying about for several weeks if it was needed. We did move our bedroll further back into the shadows to stay out of the ring of light that sprang forth from the fire so we would sleep in the shadows of the night.

The night was beautiful and had that soft Rocky Mountain chill to it and as I was watching the stars as they did their nightly twinkle and dance, Walk With Ghost stood and slowly undressed, wearing only moon shadows. My Lord, she was beautiful when she was one with nature. She was looking me full in the eye when she slowly lowered herself. I knew I was going to have to rely on Spirit's senses to warn us on any close danger since we were going to be distracted.

CHAPTER 31

Waking before dawn, I studied the surrounding forest and the campsite for anything out of kilter. Spirit was grazing in the mountain spring grass not five yards away, seeming content with no sense of alarm. Feeling that nothing was amiss, I slowly moved out from under the blankets and out from Walk With Ghost's arms and made my way to the almost dead campfire. Taking a small stick, I stirred the ashes and remaining embers until the morning air gave the fire new life and a small fire started to dance. I added some kindling to strengthen the fire and then small logs until I had a good cook fire going.

Walk With Ghost joined me and without speaking, I indicated I was going to check the jump traps and check the perimeter of our camp. Everything we did from this moment forward, we had to assume we were in perilous territory. We had no idea how close those that meant us harm were from our position here at the top of Kenosha Pass.

Making sure I was armed with my Bowie knife and a fully loaded Colt pistol, I grabbed my Winchester and melted into the still darkened evergreen and aspens. Wearing my moccasins, I could feel every twig and leaf as I moved silently through the trees to the first jump trap.

After checking and resetting all three traps, we had a bountiful two or more snowshoe rabbits and one skinny squirrel for our meals today.

Moving quickly through the trees, I found myself just outside of the campsite, but still in the shadows. I gave the pre-arranged signal to Walk With Ghost as I mimicked the sound of a mountain chickadee. She mimicked the mountain bird sound back to me so that I knew it was safe to enter the campsite without her shooting me. We had been using the sound of a mountain chickadee for over 30 years now as our signal that all was well.

As the sun made its way above the trees to the east and the darkness surrendered to the light, it started to glisten on the morning dew that clung to the tree limbs. The air was thin and cool, but felt invigorating when you drank it in. The sky was full of big fluffy white clouds that were made for looking at rather than rain or snow. It was the start of another beautiful day here near the top of Kenosha Pass.

After cleaning the rabbits and squirrel, I handed them off to Walk With Ghost to roast on the fire for our breakfast. After taking out my binoculars, I began to study the trail and the trees that stretched out below for any type of movement.

Seeing for now only the movement of the birds and squirrels as they went about living their life here in the mountains, I realized that the boredom was about to begin as we waited to see if those that wanted me were still on our trail.

Patience and perseverance were a learned trait that most did not master in their lifetime. Mountain men and Indians learned both patience and perseverance when they were young or they did not survive in the Rocky Mountains. One needed to learn how to wait life out until the right moment when action was needed. In battle it was difficult to control the emotions that flowed through your body like a raging river as you waited in patience for the right moment to strike. Once that moment presented itself, you needed not to hesitate and with all the fury that you could muster and in a blinding frenzy unleash hell onto your adversary and foe. This way of thinking and philosophy of life had kept me alive all these years. I just hoped that the last few years had not softened me...that I still had what it took...that I still had the skills that made "Ghost" the feared warrior that he was.

Walk With Ghost brought me my breakfast of roasted rabbit, beans, and campfire tortillas while I watched the trail down below. At this moment of time we had taken on the traditional roles of a man and woman; she took care of the camp and Spirit as I prepared for the battle that would eventually be forthcoming. Not that I was not capable of doing camp chores nor was Walk With Ghost not capable of being a warrior, it was just we did what we both did best for our survival. Life was dangerous and difficult enough in this high mountain frontier without having to squabble about who was going to do the camp dishes.

At mid-morning Walk With Ghost went into the woods to look for something to eat with our supper tonight besides beans and she came back with enough dandelions to make soup, pine needles for pine needle tea, and even some wild onions which were sort of a surprise since the higher in altitude, the less chance of finding these wonderfully delicious onions. We would feast like kings tonight.

The day at the top of Kenosha Pass moved slowly as I kept watching the trail below and it was about midday that I spotted movement and adjusting my binoculars, I zeroed in on Doug Webb bounty hunter and his famous mare Cimarron.

It was obvious that Doug Webb was a better than average tracker to be able to locate our trail, especially after the thunderstorm that rocked this area just a couple of days ago. Watching him from the distance, I was now struck by how much Webb reminded me of...well me. He was younger by 15 years or so, but we were about the same size and build and had the same color of pure white hair and by the way he was working the trail looking for signs, he looked and reacted just like I would. A younger version of me chasing an older version of me did not sit well in my gut.

Doug Webb was just as I knew he would be - a formidable foe. I would be a fool not to believe that a life and death struggle was about to begin with the one and only Doug Webb and

Cimarron. I tried to bury it in my heart and mind, but fear kept creeping forward. Fear was not something I had ever experienced much in my life and I knew it was not fear of living or dying but instead fear of protecting the only woman I had ever loved.

Webb and Cimarron were working the trail and it would be several hours before he got close enough to be any threat. Knowing the late afternoon and evening would be tense, I signaled Walk With Ghost to make us something to eat. I had a feeling we would be too busy later to make supper.

Walk With Ghost had already made dandelion soup and pine needle tea to go along with the roasted squirrel and rabbit. We ate in silence as we watched Doug Webb move in and out of the tree line working the trail in our direction.

At mid-afternoon and when Webb was about 400 yards out, we made sure that Walk With Ghost's weapons were all loaded once again just to make sure. At 300 yards out, I had Webb several times in my sights and could not pull the trigger, for I was not the variety of man that would kill a man from a distance with this type of shot even though I knew that Doug Webb was just that sort of man and would not have a second thought about pulling the trigger on me.

At roughly 200 yards out and after watching Doug Webb approach, he suddenly looked in my direction and pulled his rifle from his scabbard and dropped off the back of Cimarron. It took a second to register, but the bounty hunter had made our position, probably from a glint or the reflection of the glass of my binoculars. As soon as the thought of how he made our position crossed my mind, he fired his rifle and just a split second later I dropped my binoculars as rock fragments riddled my face as his 44 slug ricocheted off the top of the wall. Falling backwards and with instinct, I put out my right arm to break the fall, and my arm buckled under the weight as I hit hard.

I pushed off with my right arm again, and it buckled once again. Looking at my arm, I now could see the blood start to seep through the buckskin sleeve. Seeing the blood and now feeling the pain as it started to ebb down from the top of my right shoulder to my right hand, I realized the son of a bitch shot me! It had to be the luckiest shot of all time or he was the greatest rifle shot on the frontier; either way that son of bitch bounced one off the wall and pierced the top of my right shoulder.

Trying to move the fingers on my right hand proved to be non-productive and I had lost most of my strength in my right arm. Since I was right handed, this was not good news - not good news at all.

CHAPTER 32

Walk With Ghost moved in quickly and fired off two rounds from her Winchester in the general direction of Webb, which should give him the impression it was me firing which would cover the fact that I was wounded.

My face was bleeding almost as badly as my shoulder wound from the rock fragments from the bullet's ricochet. Thankfully I had not caught any of the rock chips in either of my eyes. My fingers on my right hand still functioned, but were responding slowly to my thought process. Balling my right fist shot a dagger of pain all the way from the wound in my shoulder to the tip of my fingers. The pain was so intense I almost passed out.

As I was trying to figure out how badly I was wounded, Walk With Ghost after firing her two rounds went quickly to gather some tree moss to plug the wound in my shoulder.

As Walk With Ghost cleansed my wounds and stuffed the puncture in the top of my shoulder with tree moss, I spoke to my wife in a calm voice, "Webb now knows where we are, and he will make his move towards us tonight. He will move slowly using all his woodcraft since he does not know I am wounded and he will be concerned that I will be stalking him in the woods. Make no mistake, men like Webb - this is what they live for."

The look of concern on Walk With Ghost's face told me all I needed to know. She was worried and the wound I had received was severe. She helped me stand and the pain made me buckle and I almost went down. Finally getting my feet beneath me, I realized that we were in deep, deep trouble.

The option of flight with one horse would only delay the encounter several hours at most. The blood loss I had already experienced and the blood I would lose in the coming hours would only weaken my condition. Looking at my wife knowing now the odds were no longer in our favor, I spoke to her in a calm voice, "Honey, I need you to take Spirit now and head to Redemption Valley and do not stop no matter what you hear. I will wait here for the bounty hunter and once I am through with him, I will meet up with you in our valley in a couple of days."

Walk With Ghost shook her head "no" as she held me in a hug before she spoke, "Don't bullshit me Matt Lee. You are in no shape to face the bounty hunter alone and if it is meant that we both die here at the top of Kenosha Pass, then so be it. I am not going anywhere without you; I stand by your side and we will fight this bastard. I love you more than the moon itself and if this is our last day and night together, then I am okay with that."

Holding her tight and shaking my head "yes," I knew that having this woman in my life was the best thing that had ever happened to me. I have always known that, and she made me proud of what she just said. She had always been one to ride the river with. Speaking calmly I told my wife, "If you are staying, we need to gather some firewood and lots of it. I want to have a rip roaring fire to distort his night vision when he comes into the camp tonight. We will stay in the shadows and let him come to us."

The plan was weak and I knew it when dealing with such an adversary as Doug Webb. I tried to put on a forceful front for Walk With Ghost, but I knew that the outcome of our encounter with the famed bounty hunter would have to have a degree of good luck for us to come out the victor. Catching a ricochet did not bode well for

Walk With Ghost and myself and it bothered me that I was now in the position of not being able to protect the one I love.

As Walk With Ghost gathered firewood, I moved cautiously back to the wall and our perimeter to see if I could catch Webb as he advanced. Since my right arm was not working and I could not grasp anything, I discarded my Winchester and held my Colt in my left hand.

There was only about an hour left before sundown and the sun had already disappeared behind a cloud bringing a gloomy cast to the end of the day. The air was still but growing colder as the warmth of the sun was now blocked by the increasing cloud cover. Walk With Ghost had gathered more than enough wood for our fire tonight, and I indicated with a nod of my head to go ahead and start the fire.

The pain in my shoulder caused by Webb's ricochet had now finally settled as a dull throb that was tolerable. I had been weakened by the blood loss, but the tree moss stuffed in my wound had now completely stopped the flow of blood. My fingers and arm were slow to respond to any type of movement. I knew I was in no shape to fight one such as the bounty hunter that was stalking me. I also realized that there was no choice in the matter; we would either live through the night or Doug Webb would. It was that simple.

Seeing movement out of the corner of my eye, not that of the bounty hunter out in the woods but that of Walk With Ghost, I turned to watch my wife as she went about making the fire larger than normal and taking care of Spirit our mare. With the possibility of death just a couple of hundred yards away, it got me to thinking about life - my life and the life that Walk With Ghost and I have had. If death finds us here on top of this lonely mountain this evening, I was at peace with that. We had a good run and our love for one another had never faltered. My whole life since the battle on Marble Mountain at the haunted La Caverna Del Oro when all my friends had been killed 30 years ago had been a near death experience. The Rocky Mountain frontier was not for the weak hearted and it was an honorable place to die. I was ready, we were ready, and on this night on top of Kenosha Pass, the famous bounty hunter Webb will know he had been in the fight of his life.

As the sun finally dipped down below the horizon and the darkness started to close in on the mountain, I heard Cimarron the Appaloosa mare that belonged to Webb snort and stomp her foot not far in the distance down the slope, which meant nothing in terms of where Webb was. More likely than not he had left Cimarron and was moving on foot in our direction.

Now that the darkness had fallen and taken hold of the night, my eyesight could only reach as far as the campfire light. Walk With Ghost helped me as we moved back into the shadows just above our campfire.

My wound had weakened me to the point that I was having trouble walking and even the act of holding my Winchester and Colt pistol was proving difficult. Of course Webb did not know that I was wounded and right now that was about the only advantage that we had. Walk With Ghost would fight to the death if needed, and I was proud to call her my wife.

I tried to stay alert, but the wound and the tension of the day were now taking a toll on me. Walk With Ghost was doing her best to be the warrior that I needed to be.

The fire was a full blaze as the last logs that Walk With Ghost had added before we retreated into the shadows had caught and were burning intensely. As we waited and watched the perimeter of the ring of light that flooded our camp, we searched for any movement or sign that Webb was close. We took care not to look directly at the fire for fear it would cause us night blindness.

Time moved slowly as the seconds turned to minutes and then into several hours. Neither Walk With Ghost nor I had any luck in detecting any movement in the woods, nor any sounds. The night sounds had disappeared from the top of Kenosha Pass with no crickets, owls, or the constant buzz of the bugs at night. It was as if the whole mountain knew what was to come and was waiting.

Spirit gave us the first indication of Webb's whereabouts as she snorted and then looked in our direction. While trying to decipher what Spirit was trying to tell us, she once again snorted several times and pawed the ground with her hoof and looked directly at us...no, not at us, but up above us.

It dawned on me that the bounty hunter had gotten around us and had been moving down the mountain towards us. I quickly spun to look behind us when I heard the twig from underfoot snap. Webb was not only behind us, but almost on top of us.

CHAPTER 33

What was astonishing was that as Webb had been using his stealth and woodcraft to move towards our camp, in the darkness and the low light of the cloud covered moon, he had not known our exact position until I turned to face him. He was just as surprised as I was that he was so close to us. By close - I mean a couple of feet.

Trying to stand in an abrupt motion to aim my pistol from my left hand proved to be my undoing. In my wounded condition I was no longer agile enough to make any quick or sudden moves. My body and mind just were not up to the challenge. Webb did not know I was already wounded and his first instinct was to rush me drawing his Bowie knife in his right hand.

Webb also had the advantage as he was rushing downhill, which gave him all the momentum in his attack. Webb's headlong battle rush caused me to drop my Colt and brought the bounty hunter chest to chest with me and sent us both tumbling ass over heels with both of us locked in a death grip with my only good arm and hand holding off Webb's bowie knife as he tried to plunge it into my chest.

We plummeted in such a manner for three full rolls before the momentum gave way and the force of our downward plunge separated us when we landed on an outcropping ledge just above the campfire below. We were separated, but still rolling when both of us were pitched off of the granite outcropping and landed in what was Walk With Ghost's and my campsite.

The sudden stop of hitting the flat ground beneath the outcropping took the air right out of my lungs. Having landed on my wounded shoulder and arm was probably the only thing that kept me from passing out because the pain that shuddered through my body made every joint and muscle scream with agony.

Trying to roll to my feet or my knees was proving to be an epic failure as my body was not functioning when my mind told it to move. Spitting out dirt and pine needles, I moved my head from side to side trying to locate Webb.

Locating Webb proved to be easy. After plunging off the outcropping he landed in the campfire and set himself ablaze. The fringe on his buckskin shirt as well as his snow white hair had been ignited before he was able to free himself from the burning logs. Webb, once out of the fire, had dropped to the ground to do the fire roll to extinguish the flames. I saw all of this as I lay wounded on my back in the dirt trying to force my body to move.

My limbs only felt the pain caused by my wounds and the downward tumble as I was dropped like a sack of potatoes in this spot I now found myself. Closing my eyes, I said a silent prayer for my limbs to regain some sort of movement. Concentrating on my left arm, I started to feel a blood rush as my fingers and hand started to move. In seconds I was able to move my left arm again. Once some sort of normal feeling was present, I pushed myself into a kneeling position keeping my eyes always on my adversary as he was battling his own problems after being set afire.

Checking that I still had my Bowie knife, I tried to stand knowing the bounty hunter, although burnt some, was still in the fight; Doug Webb was not beaten yet - not by a long shot.

Finally gaining my feet, I tried my right arm again and it was dead to the world. No matter how much I wished it to be so, there was no movement whatsoever. My right arm was useless in any encounter that would come. I struggled to pull my Bowie knife from the sheath that was strapped on my right side with my left hand. Once gaining a hold of my Bowie, I held it in an upward grip.

Webb had finally put himself out and he stood with remarkable speed for a man that just a second ago was being roasted alive.

Amazingly Webb was still holding onto his Bowie knife after all that had transpired and had it in his right hand as he turned to face me. I could still see the smoke coming off the bounty hunter's hair in the dancing light and shadows of the campfire. Other than being somewhat burnt, he seemed to be in way better shape than I was in, for all of his movements showed no signs of any type of injury. He had not been slowed down by the tumble down the mountain, which did not bode well for Walk With Ghost's and my survival. Walk With Ghost? In the fight and tumble from the mountainside, I had lost track of Walk With Ghost. Right now I had to push thoughts of her to the back of my mind as Webb started to advance on me with his Bowie.

As we started to circle each other, it became evident to Webb that I was wounded and in a bad way. So much so a huge grin appeared on his face as he spoke to me, "Hell, Matt Lee looks like you are all done in, old man. The mighty warrior "Ghost" seems to have lost his fighting edge. I think now I will kill you slow and carve you up into little pieces…except your head, I need that to get me $2000. You had your run old man, but you are no longer king of the Rocky Mountain frontier. All I ever heard since coming to these mountains was how you became a legend. Look at you now 'Ghost!' You are weak and your time on mother earth is just about to an end."

As I stumbled in our circle of death with all my weakness, I knew that my life was about over and I felt no fear, for to die a warrior's death was actually preferable rather than dying in my sleep from old age. Doug Webb, as evil as the bastard was, also happened to be one tough son of a bitch and to die at his hand would not be a dishonor. Speaking with no fear, because I felt none, "Son it is not over till it is over. I actually sort of respected you as a tough man, a warrior, until this moment. I never realized you jawed and talked your foes to death. You think you are the better man Webb? I am not done yet; I am still walking."

The insult was not one of my better ones, but it seemed to inspire Webb to shut his mouth and get on with it. He moved in close, thrusting with his right hand testing my reaction time. I moved with dimwitted slowness and stumbled which brought another smile to the bounty hunter's face.

Webb moved more quickly the next time and sliced with his Bowie which found the flesh of my left arm as his Bowie slashed my buckskin shirt and cut deep into my left shoulder before he quickly moved away. Guess he was at least a man of his word when he said he was going to cut me up into small pieces.

I was wounded and knew I was no match for a man like Webb with his fighting skills! Just as Webb started another move towards me, Walk With Ghost jumped on his back and started to rake with all her strength at his left eye with her fingernails.

Moving as fast as I could which was not fast at all, I tried to take advantage of what Walk With Ghost had given me. I stumbled in and with an upward thrust stabbed Webb as he struggled with Walk With Ghost, who was latched onto the bounty hunter's back in a death grip.

My stab and thrust had not been true since I had tried for the center of his rib cage where his heart would be and either through bad timing, weakened muscles, or the Lord's will, I only accomplished stabbing him in his side, not the death blow I was hoping for - a wound for sure, but not an instant death wound.

Webb was able to punch me and push me backwards with his left hand. The punch was hard enough in my weakened condition to send me backwards until I stumbled and landed once again in the dirt on my behind. He then sought and got a hold of Walk With Ghost's hair with his right hand.

Webb, after freeing himself of me, brought Walk With Ghost violently over his shoulder by her hair and spun her to face him and hit her so hard in the face with his fist that when her body slumped and dropped to the ground, I was afraid that he had killed her with that one punch.

Walk With Ghost's raking of Webb's eye would leave him forever marked for life which I felt was fitting for having messed with my wife. I struggled to get up; however, my legs and arms were having none of it as my muscles once again decided they were not going to respond. Webb, after a few seconds of checking his wounds on his face and the stab wound in his side, started to move angrily towards me. If I was going to die in the next minutes, I did find some enjoyment in the fact we had made the famed bounty madder than all get out.

I could smell the burnt and dirty leather of his moccasin as he kicked me with all his strength in the head, repeatedly. After each kick, I almost passed out only to be reawakened with the next kick. The son of a bitch was going to kick me to death and there was not a thing I could do about it.

Webb kicked me in the head so many times he wore himself out and had to stop to rest with his hands on his knees. After resting for a short spell, he was still breathing hard as he searched the ground looking for his Bowie knife that he had dropped during his fight with Walk With Ghost and myself.

My mind was a blur and aflutter as I struggled to try and keep my wits about me as darkness and death loomed not far in the corner of my mind. My whole life started to spin in my mind like shuffling cards. Everyone whom I cared for and loved were present here now in the last seconds of my life and in my mind. I could see their faces sharp and clear - Sam, Dan, Mike, Jay, Lucas, Devon, Sherol, Roger, Kellie Shawn, Chance, Piah, and of course the woman who had given my life meaning, Walk With Ghost.

Webb with his foot rolled me over onto my back and with a foot on each side of my battered torso, he sat down hard on me and raised his Bowie knife with both fists over his head to deliver the final killing strike.

Looking in my eyes, Webb the bounty hunter saw no fear.

The shotgun blast startled me almost as much as it startled Webb. The difference was that Webb had taken the bulk of it in his face.

CHAPTER 34

T he momentum of the shotgun blast forced Webb's body to fall backwards into a dead heap of what use to be the bounty hunter on top of my legs.

My mind struggled and strained to stay awake and not black out. The numerous kicks to my head and upper body had taken their toll and death was not far away. I could almost feel the presence of the Specter of Death with his long blade sickle as he waited just out of sight waiting to take me to heaven or hell. I could only be so lucky if it was heaven that awaited me, but more than likely it was hell that had a claim on my soul.

My mind was all aflutter and my eyes were filled with running blood from more than a dozen wounds to my face and top of my noggin from the ricochet and foot stomping. I tried to blink to clear my eyes to see; it was almost more than I could handle, but it was proving to be a classic failure on my part.

My mind started to clear a tad since the boot stomping had stopped and I could feel the dead weight of Webb lying on my legs; I tried to push him off with my legs, but my body was so injured from the abuse it had taken in the last several hours I could not muster enough strength to shake off the dead bounty hunter.

I thought it must have been Walk With Ghost who had killed the bounty hunter, but… wait a minute. The more I rolled it around in my scattered brain pan, I realized we didn't have a shotgun. I chuckled a little to myself thinking the bounty hunter and his kicking my head probably did more damage than spending a night in that faraway haunted La Caverna Del Oro. My brains had to be scrambled for sure I decided.

As I was blinking and trying to clear my vision and deciphering how badly my brains had been tossed, I felt the weight of the bounty hunter being lifted off my legs and heard a voice that somehow penetrated the fog in my brain, "I don't reckon there is much left of you for the soldier boys to hang Matt Lee."

The voice belonged to the Territorial Marshal Eric Robert. Speaking in a weak and hoarse voice I replied, "My wife? How is Walk With Ghost?"

Bending over me so I could focus in on his face, "Still out, but I made her as comfortable as I could. She seems to be breathing fine and I believe she will wake up in time with no noticeable side effects from her encounter with the bounty hunter. You, I am not so sure about. You are a mess Matt Lee. Looks to me as if you are just on the edge of death, but I have been wrong before."

The Marshal reached down and tilted my head so I could sip some cool creek water from his canteen, and I got to say it was the tastiest water I had ever had.

Soon as he was done giving me a drink, he poured some water on a piece of cloth that he produced from his back pocket and started to dab and clean the wounds on my face. The cold water felt wonderful, but the minute he pressed with his fingers into my flesh to wash some of the blood off my face, the pain and shooting stars shuddered my body and then total blackness flooded my awareness.

The "caw, caw" of a magpie in the evergreen tree above my head woke me up. I shifted my weight to find a more comfortable spot to lay on the bed made from evergreen limbs spread out on the ground and when I could not find a suitable position, I gave up. My head hurt like hell and feeling it some with my swollen fingers on my left hand, I could feel that it was twice the size as before. The good news was, even though my face was swollen, I could see daylight through a small thin line in between my eyelids. My mind seemed to be clear since I was thinking rationally, so my brains were not totally scrambled. Once I established I was still alive, thinking somewhat clearly, and not blind, I tried then to take a survey of the remaining parts and pieces of my body.

After some concentrated effort and a considerable amount of pain, I realized I could move both arms, legs, toes, and fingers. I also thanked the stars and the good Lord since I knew this was a win-win since I had taken rock fragments to my face, a piercing wound to my shoulder from a ricochet, an ass over heels tumble from a mountainside, a knife wound to my left arm, and a severe boot stomping to my head. And if all of that was not enough for me to feel my age, then it was this damn headache that wanted to pound a hole in the front of my face. But, by golly, I was still alive.

After realizing my good luck, I was able to roll over on my side without the pain causing me to pass out and I saw Eric Robert sitting on a log eating what looked like some roasted rabbit on a spit. Then my angel, my wife, my lover came into my view holding a canteen and I tried to speak, but it came out as some sort of mumble, "Walk With Ghost, I am glad you are okay."

Walk With Ghost was not more than ten yards away when I spoke and at first she turned towards me and stared as her mind was trying to ponder that I actually said something. Once she realized her eyes and ears were not playing a trick, her eyes flooded with tears and a huge smile appeared to split her face in two as she moved quickly towards me. Her voice broke with emotion as she spoke, "Matt Lee you had me worried as all get out. This is the first time you have spoken in six days."

I attempted to smile, but my face was not having any of that; however, I was able to get out a small chuckle, "Six days? Honey, I thought you were mad at me for getting my butt whooped and all and I just could not bring myself to talk to you."

Walk With Ghost kneeled down so she could lovingly touch my face with her fingertips. Still with tears in her eyes and smile on her face, she said with a small laugh, "You can be such an ass

Matt Lee. I have seen my man at his worst and I still think you are the best and I love you more than anything."

Her words always had a way of making me love her more if that was even possible. I reached out and grabbed her hand to hold. Her face had taken a beating from when the bounty hunter had punched her. Even though she had six days to heal some, it still looked painful. Both eyes were still black and blue and her nose was misshapen some and probably would always have a lean to the left for the rest of her life. If Webb was not already dead, I would kill the man for touching my wife in such a manner.

Walk With Ghost rolled me back over onto my back and I was in no shape to argue with her. The movement caused me a great deal of pain. Once on my back, she grabbed my head and tilted it upwards as she let me drink from the canteen she had just got done filling before I woke up. The cool creek water felt refreshing and tasty as I took a couple of huge gulps of the life-giving water. After having my fill for now, I nodded my head in the direction of Eric Robert who was slowly striding towards Walk With Ghost and myself. "I take it, it was the Marshal who killed the bounty hunter?"

Walk With Ghost was still stroking my face gingerly with the back of her fingers when she replied, "Yes, it was. I didn't see it exactly, but it was done when I woke up after being knocked out. The Marshal saved both of our lives."

Territorial Marshal Eric Robert, the man who saved my wife's life and my own, stopped a couple of feet short of me and squatted down to the ground as an Indian would do. He had a long stem of mountain wheat grass he was chewing on when he smiled and spoke with some laughter, "I guess I owe your lovely wife two bits; I bet her the first words out of your mouth if you ever woke up would be "water" and she bet it would be her name."

Turning to look at the man whom I respected, "Why did you kill Webb? He had every legal right to kill me and claim the bounty money."

The smile slowly evaporated off the Marshal's face and he looked as if he was pondering my question some before he spoke, "I guess I'm really not sure why other than I reacted to the situation. In the few seconds after riding in, I took all in account what my mind had told me was happening, and I saw Walk With

Ghost lying in a heap and out cold and you were at that moment defenseless, and Webb was having no second thoughts about stabbing you in the heart. I just grabbed my Greener shotgun loaded with double ought buck and shot him. Thinking back on it, the truth of the matter is I never liked Webb, and I sort of like you."

Shaking my head "yes" in understanding, "I reckon I understand that Marshal. My next question is what happens now?"

Marshal Eric Robert slowly stood and without a smile on his face replied, "I have a duly sworn arrest warrant from the territorial office in Denver and I aim to fulfill my sworn duty. Matt Lee I am taking you in. You are under arrest for murder."

CHAPTER 35

S haking my head in understanding, I had already known the answer. Marshal Eric Robert was a man who once given a job would never shy away from doing what needed to be done whether he liked it or not. He was bullheaded like that and I for one admired it. "I guess Marshal, I knew that was going to be the answer. I will go willingly and peacefully with you to Denver even though I know those soldier boys are going to hang me no matter what. I am much obliged that you came to Walk With Ghost's rescue. I give you my word of honor that you will get no trouble from me on the trail."

Marshal nodded his head "yes" and gave a small chuckle. "I was hoping you would say that since I reckon I did not want to handcuff and shackle the man or the legend that the Utes called "Ghost." It would go against my grain to have to do that to someone that I admire as much as you Matt Lee. That being said, I am thinking a few more days here to help you recover enough to be able to travel."

With the Marshal watching and tracking all of our movements, he watched as Walk With Ghost sat down beside me and with tears in her eyes started to apply some healing pine needle salve to my wounds. Reaching out and gently wiping a tear from her face, "Don't cry for me my love. Who knows, maybe they will set me free. I reckon Redemption Valley will have to wait for a spell."

Walk With Ghost's face showed what her heart knew to be true. The sorrow on her face told the story that we both knew and that was there was no way in hell that the U.S. Cavalry were going to let me walk away from killing those four troopers in Grand Lake. Touching her face once again and turning it so she had to look me in the eyes, "Honey, we still have these few days right now while I am getting healed up. No use fretting about the storm in the future; let's enjoy the freedom and sunshine now."

Walk With Ghost buried her head into my chest. "I love loving you Matt Lee, My whole life has been better since you saved me from the lion so many years ago. I cannot imagine living without you. It seems I could not love you any more than I do right now, but I know tomorrow I will love you even more my husband."

I closed my eyes and held her tight. No more words needed to pass between us now. We both knew that we had been meant for each other over the years.

Eric Robert watched the whole exchange and I was not embarrassed to show my love for my wife in front of him. I wondered if he had been so blessed in his life to have what Walk With Ghost and I had. Not sure if the Marshal understood or even cared as his face was empty of emotion as he turned to walk back to the campfire to finish his supper.

Another seven days passed at our campsite near the top of Kenosha Pass as I regained all movement in both my arms and legs as the mountain air helped speed my recovery. That being said, even after 13 days of healing with the lofty air of the high mountains, I was still having discomfort just trying to sit up. Walking, even though I had regained all movement, was a whole different matter altogether because each step jarred some bruised and battered muscle or bone that was far from being anywhere close to normal. I also started to feel the need to get on with it, whatever it was.

The last week had been the typical fair weather one might expect in the high mountains during the spring with the days warm and the nights cool. As much as I loved having these few days with Walk With Ghost, the future was causing me considerable dismay and I was starting to tire of the wait. Marshal Eric Robert seemed in no real hurry and content to give me as much time as I needed but after speaking to him, we decided it was time to move on towards Denver and the hangman's noose that probably awaited me there.

Right after saving mine and Walk With Ghost's life, the Marshal had buried the bounty hunter's body in a shallow grave, but only after he had cut Webb's head off and put it in an old sugar sack. To try and keep the head as fresh as possible, the Marshal left the sugar sack in some shade in a hollow of an old evergreen. Webb's head would be used in Denver for identification as to what had happened to the famous bounty hunter. I rolled it around some in my thoughts and thought it was best that nobody know that the Marshal had killed Webb in the manner that it had happened. Eric Robert thought differently of course being the man that he was. His thoughts were it should be stated to those that were the law of the land exactly what happened here on this mountain. I worried that he may face some sort of charges himself for killing Webb. The decapitation may have seemed brutal and downright horrifying to those that were not accustomed to the hardships and life of the Rocky Mountain frontier, but to men such as the Marshal and myself, it was business as usual.

After our typical supper of roasted rabbit and campfire tortillas, Walk With Ghost fell fast asleep with her head buried in my chest. From my vantage point I was able to observe the Marshal as he stared towards the darkness of the night, puffing away on his corncob pipe. He seemed to be in some deep thought and my observation was that he was a troubled man.

In the last week I had learned very little about the Marshal other than he hailed from the Black Hills of the Dakota Territory from a town called Belle Fourche. He spoke some about a wife and son that had died. Walk With Ghost and I had learned all of that in the first day, but after that the Marshal made it a point not to speak of such things to us. I knew it was his way of dealing with the fact that he actually cared for Walk With Ghost and myself. He could not be our friends and had to distance himself from us and his duty and job. I respected that and left the conversation between us only about what needed to be said.

Looking down into the sleeping face of my wife, I thought of all that she had done for me in the last couple of weeks in getting me healed from my encounter with the bounty hunter. I held her a little tighter and silently mouthed, "I love you" before I drifted off to sleep.

Gunfire woke me out of a dead sleep and I tried to react, but my body was still healing and was slow to respond. The Marshal reacted much faster and had drawn his Colt and had backed into the shadows away from the glowing embers of our dying campfire. I patted myself down looking for my weapons before I realized due to the circumstances I was not armed. After some difficulty I was able to stand on my own as Walk With Ghost and I followed the Marshal's lead and slowly moved into the shadows as I listened to the night.

Four more gunshots rang out and the sound echoed through the night, overcoming the slight wind and the "tree whispers." Eric Robert in a hushed tone spoke, "How far Matt Lee?"

In a quiet but assured voice I replied, "Two miles, maybe more, but not much. I think to the east towards the bottom of Kenosha. I remember seeing a cabin and smelling the cook fire of some homesteaders. Walk With Ghost and I gave them a wide berth avoiding anyone we could. I think those shots came from that direction."

The Marshal had moved back in towards our dying campfire and sat down on a log and proceeded to tamp some tobacco into his corncob pipe. Pointing toward Walk With Ghost and myself, "You and your wife try and get some more sleep. I will take the first watch."

Realizing that the dawn was only about an hour or so away, there would only be one watch. The Marshal seemed content to smoke his pipe and wait out the darkness, so I grabbed my wife's hand and headed back to our bedroll.

Lying down, neither of us went to sleep and we both watched the three horses. Spirit my mare and the Marshal's mare Creek had started to graze again. The last remaining horse was the bounty hunter's mare Cimarron who seemed to be on silent alert. Then of course Cimarron always seemed on alert.

CHAPTER 36

After a cold breakfast of elk jerky and campfire tortillas, we watched another glorious Rocky Mountain sunrise that painted the sky with glowing orange and blue hues that to my knowledge no painter or artist had been able to duplicate.

It was also at daybreak that we had noticed the dark curling smoke to the east and down below us at the bottom of Kenosha Pass. Something was set afire in the same direction as the gunshots we heard before sunup.

The Marshal watched the smoke in the distance as he finished his early morning pull on his corncob pipe without saying anything. He was doing some heavy thinking and I could almost smell the burning oil as the gears in his mind were working double time.

It had been decided that Walk With Ghost would ride Spirit and I would ride the bounty hunter's horse Cimarron. Walk With Ghost's petite frame made her unlikely she could handle the tall and muscular horse. Hell, in my weakened condition I was not so sure I could handle the famous horse.

Walk With Ghost and I had Cimarron and Spirit saddled and we watched as Eric Robert retrieved the sugar sack and Webb's head and secured it in his saddle bag on his horse Creek. The Marshal also unpacked my gun belt, Colt, and both Walk With Ghost's and my Winchesters and slowly made his way towards me. After handing them to me, he said in a serious tone, "You promised to not give me any trouble on the trail and I know you and Walk With Ghost will honor that Matt Lee. That promise only carries water with me and not to anyone that we might run across on the trail. It is my duty and obligation to find out where those gunshots came from and what was set on fire and it just so happens you and your wife will have to tag along. I reckon it does not feel right having you ride in possible harm's way without your weapons."

Without another word the Marshal spun on his heels and headed back to mount his horse Creek. After belting on my Colt, I palmed it several times, and it flowed into my hand like water, maybe not as fast as I use to be, but it sure felt good to have it strapped on. It made me feel whole; it is funny how a sidearm becomes a part of you like another hand. It just felt right.

After placing both Winchesters in the saddle scabbards, Walk With Ghost easily mounted Spirit, and both she and the Marshal got a chuckle as I tried to mount Cimarron. It was only after several attempts that I was able to mount myself squarely in the saddle to the amusement of all, even Cimarron herself, who kept looking back at me like "Who is this fool?" I had a feeling it would not be long before Cimarron tried to show me who was boss.

As we moved out towards the bottom of Kenosha in the direction of Denver, the Marshal took point followed by Walk With Ghost. Lowering myself to speak quietly to Cimarron, "Work with me Cimarron and we will get along fine, and just remember your last owner is riding with the Marshal with his head in a sugar sack."

Cimarron tossed her head twice and snorted. Not sure if she had agreed to our deal or not as I gave her a slight jab of my spur and brought up the rear of our column as we moved out.

As sore as my body was and knowing how stiff all my muscles and joints were going to be after the end of the day, it did feel good to be back in the saddle. Cimarron was the most muscled and powerful horse I had ever ridden. The legendary horse was said to have great stamina and staying power and after just a few minutes in the saddle on this beast, I knew that to be true. She had not tried to buck me off yet, which was a good thing, because if she wanted me off her back, there would be no way in hell I would have been able to stop her. Horses such as Cimarron you did not master or control - you and the horse came to an understanding is all.

As we moved in the direction of where we had heard the gunshots and saw the black smoke, I could not help but think Walk With Ghost and I were riding in the wrong direction and away from Redemption Valley. As if she could read my mind, Walk With Ghost turned in her saddle and looked not at me, but above and beyond back towards the top of Kenosha Pass. Knowing my wife so well, I could read the sorrow that her face showed as we moved away from the direction that was to be our final home. Redemption Valley was just a two day ride southwest from the top of Kenosha Pass through the South Park basin to Boreas Pass. It broke my heart to see such sadness. Walk With Ghost deserved better than an uncertain future.

Each step that Cimarron took and the constant pain that my body was experiencing reminded me how close to death I had been. It was difficult to take my mind off of the pain and focus on what lay ahead.

What lay ahead was just a short trip down the trail to see what all the shooting and ruckus was about in the couple of hours before daylight. Pushing to the back of my brain pan the possibility of a hangman's noose waiting for me in Denver, I set my mind to focus on the moment at hand.

After the boot stomping Webb had done on my noggin as he tried to kick me to death left me some struggles in thinking clearly, but it seemed to be getting better. Even in the days when the madness had taken hold after the ill-fated trip to Marble Mountain and the haunted La Caverna Del Oro, I still had the clarity of mind to understand the dangers all around me in the wilderness. My age, getting shot and stabbed, a tumble down the mountain, and getting my butt whooped were not agreeing with me at all. I had to chuckle at the absurdity of it all. Walk With Ghost turned to look at me with a quizzical look and I waved it off. Laughing out loud this time I thought, "She must think I am touched in the head."

It was not long before we found what the Marshal was looking for. We sat on the horses just inside the aspen trees that surrounded the burnt out log cabin as we surveyed the scene before us. What had happened here was already done and there was no movement or life in and around the homestead. Where we sat we could see two bodies, that of a man and a young boy. Marshal Eric Robert not looking at me directly asked, "What do you make of this Matt Lee?"

It was evident what had happened here and the Marshal already knew; he was just wanting me to confirm it. "More than likely outlaws. White men and not Indians - the bodies show no sign that renegade Indians did this. A random killing for what little these folks had. I am sure we will find they either took a woman or we will find her body in the remains of the cabin."

Marshal Eric Robert nodded his head "yes" as he gave his horse Creek some rein and headed towards the homesteaders' massacre site. "Matt Lee I would be much obliged if you scouted and figured out what direction the outlaws are headed. I will look to see if this homesteader had a good digging shovel. I have bodies to bury."

Walk With Ghost and I scouted the perimeter and located the outlaw's trail fairly easily because they were not trying to hide it thinking nobody would find their handiwork for some time. The tracks told me the story of what, when, and where, but not the why. Three men rode in from the north and they left heading due east with an extra horse which probably had belonged to that fellow that the Marshal just got done digging a grave for."

We found the woman in the cabin just as I thought we would, and she had been raped and beaten then burned. I suspected her husband and son had been killed before her abuse started. I knew the Marshal well enough by now that my trip and hanging in Denver would be delayed some as we would track down these desperadoes. I was not in much of a hurry to be hung just yet, and these scum had to be dealt with in a harsh manner.

Walk With Ghost did what she could to make the bodies more presentable for burial. We found nothing that remained in the cabin that would tell us who these folks were or where they were from. We would bury them with no names and a year from now nature and the wilderness would have claimed the wooden cross we would leave as if these poor folks had never even lived and died here. Life in general was tough, but it seemed it was even harsher here in the Rocky Mountains.

Marshal Eric Robert did all of the digging since my body was not up to the physical task, but I was able to help with the easier chore of shoveling dirt back on these poor souls that had probably made their way here hoping for a better life.

We read some of the bible not knowing if the dead had been God fearing folks and if they were what their favorite passage was. It was the best we could do during this sad time. The Marshal surprised Walk With Ghost and me as he started to belt out the song "Amazing Grace," and it was one hell of a performance that would have done that English poet John Newton that had written the hymn proud. I know it brought a tear to both Walk With Ghost's and my eyes.

As the hour of the day was only mid-afternoon, we ate a quick meal and readied our horses after making sure our weapons were clean and loaded. The Marshal even gave me back my Bowie knife for when we found the killers of this family if the fighting got up-close and personal.

Having done all we could to help these poor folks on their journey to the afterlife, we did what all righteous men do - we headed east to bring justice to those who prey upon the weak.

CHAPTER 37

The trail that the outlaws left behind was easy to follow. I had decided that these three murdering outlaws were either dumb or just plain lazy, probably both. They had made no attempt to hide their trail whatsoever.

They were moving fast though, and had a good nine to ten hour head start on us. At the pace they were moving and the pace we were able to track them, I reckoned it would be some time tomorrow when we would catch up to them. One could not forget no matter how dumb and lazy, they would still be very treacherous. Obviously the meaning of life and how sacred it is was not built into their moral fiber. Men such as this were a scourge across the frontier which is why there were such men as Territorial Marshal Eric Robert.

It would be curious how the Marshal would handle it once we located the outlaws. I for one would just kill each and every one in a fierce all out frontal attack. Of course, that type of thinking had gotten me where I am at today, looking at a hangman's noose in Denver.

Like it or not law, justice, and the courts were changing here and all around the Colorado Territory. When I first came to these mountains, justice was only as far as the end of your Hawkins Rifle or the tip of your Bowie knife and if you were man enough to serve that justice.

Men like myself were a rare breed that were going the way of the ancient Indian tribes and fast disappearing from the landscape. In a roundabout way I had begun to realize that for some spell and that is why I wanted to make my final home in Redemption Valley with Walk With Ghost to live out in peace and harmony far from people and the encroaching civilization. Those troopers I killed in Grand Lake had put a dogleg in living out our lives in our close, but faraway hidden valley. Thinking back on the killing of those troopers - regrettable as it was - I would not have done anything different.

The weather at mid-afternoon was still a pleasant Rocky Mountain spring day. The sun was arcing across an endless blue sky and the warmth of it on my face made me feel alive. My muscles were sore as all get out, and I was a long way from being healed, but by golly it was good to still be above ground. The wind was stirring the aspen leaves enough to make them quake and give us a rendition of the "tree whispers."

The Marshal knew I was a far better tracker than he was and I started riding point following the trail. Walk With Ghost and Spirit were close behind and the Marshal Eric Robert was pulling up the rear on his horse Creek.

Cimarron and I, it seemed, had come to an understanding and were working nicely with each other. I didn't try to be her boss and she didn't try to kill me; it was working out better than expected. Chuckling to myself, "Especially the part about the heavily muscled horse not killing me." Thinking that I reached down and patted her neck and she snorted in acknowledgment.

We made good time and I thought we were only about an hour to two hours behind the outlaws when we stopped for the night where Geneva Creek flowed into the north fork of the South Platte River. We had a cold camp for supper of leftover camp tortillas and elk jerky. The Marshal and I thought it best not to have the chance of the men we were chasing smelling any wood smoke. To the best of our knowledge, they did not have a clue that anyone was trailing and hunting them, and we wanted to keep it that way. We should catch up with them sometime in the morning.

If I had been all healed up, I would have put on my moccasins and used my woodcraft to sneak up on their camp in the dark. It would have been beneficial to see how they were armed and how they guarded their camp. Even though I was on the mend and it had now been two weeks from the boot stomping I took from Webb, I was far from being able to sneak up on anyone. We would just wing it once we encountered them.

Since the first day that the Marshal had saved my bacon and rescued Walk With Ghost from the bounty hunter, he spoke very little to us. And tonight he was not speaking at all. I watched him as he smoked his corncob pipe down by the river so the air current of the river would take the smell of tobacco away from the outlaws. He seemed troubled and the pained expression on his face told the story of a conflicted mind. Knowing the man for what he was, I felt his conflict was not about those we would oppose tomorrow, for that was black and white in his world. They committed a horrible crime and it was his duty to bring justice to them. If he could keep them alive, he would do that and drop them in front of a judge and jury. If they fought and we were forced to kill them, he was equally okay with that. Either way justice would have been served.

His conflict I was sure had to do with me. First off, he liked and respected me as an equal. Second, he knew that given the same circumstance with the troopers in Grand Lake that if it had been him facing it instead of me, he would do exactly what I did. In his mind, I committed no crime and had been defending my wife and her honor. A black and white situation and justice had been served. Not so simple, though with the U.S. Cavalry involved and it all became a big gray area. As an officer of the court, he would have some say at my trial if it was a civilian trial, which it most surely would not be. The U.S Cavalry was not going to let alone a man who had killed that many of its men for having some fun with an Indian squaw then shooting her after she attacked one of them. It made them look weak and sure enough they would hang me for killing those troopers if they deserved it or not. Marshal Eric

Robert knew this just as well as I did. Watching the Marshal from a distance, I wondered what the outcome of his troubled mind would be. I had made a promise I would not buck him on the trail as he took me in and my honor was at stake. Being honorable sometimes costs you your life. This was probably one of those times.

The Marshal and I cleaned and oiled our weapons before the sun completely dropped out of sight in the western horizon. The darkness started to overtake the mountainside, and the full moon made its appearance over the top of the evergreens and aspens to the east. The moon had the sky all to herself tonight because nary a cloud could be seen as far as my eyes could see.

It was decided I would take the first watch and I left Walk With Ghost as soon as she had fallen asleep. I nodded toward the Marshal and he tamped out the remaining tobacco in his corncob pipe and put his tobacco makings back into their leather pouch that he carried for that purpose. The Marshal then stood and stretched and slowly made his way to his bedroll. He stopped once and turned towards me as if to say something but changed his mind as he turned back and continued on to his bedroll.

I found a suitable spot hidden in the long shadows of the aspens created by the full moon to keep watch and guard our camp. With the outlaws so close, we did not want to be surprised ourselves.

Even though my noggin had taken such a boot stomping and I was sure the meat in my head and been swished around in my brain pan, it would seem my eyesight and hearing had not been affected in any way.

Being a man of the wilderness I had become accustomed to the sights and sounds of the night in the mountains and they all became familiar to me. The wind was slight and there was a slight quaking to the aspens which was one of the melodies of the night that I loved so much. Beyond that I could hear the water as it rushed over the rocks in the nearby river and the occasional splash of a rainbow or brown trout that had found a wayward fly to suck from the air. Beyond the moon I could glimpse what seemed as all the stars in the universe, but of course I knew that was impossible. The stars are as bright tonight as I had ever seen them, and they twinkled their white light rain that the good Lord had seen to paint them with down upon us - "diamonds in the sky" my old friend Mike Sands use to call them.

As Walk With Ghost and the Marshal were sleeping and with the real prospect that soon I would be hung until I was dead, I reflected some of my life and the adventures I have had that have brought me here to this moment in time. All in all my life and its journey had been spent almost entirely in the mountains and the wilderness. I had my ups and downs and had been led down many paths, some of which had been filled with the blood of my enemies and of that I reckon, I had no regrets. To the Ute Indians and those that understood the Rocky Mountains, I had become the legend called "Ghost" - something I never wanted nor intended to happen. My vendetta, after my friends had been massacred on Marble Mountain near the haunted La Caverna Del Oro, was what made me a legend, but it was something I was never proud of.

The thing I was most proud of was being with the woman whom I called my wife and who still cherished and loved me even with all my numerous faults. Walk With Ghost was the only thing that made my life worth anything. She was my... everything. If and when I do my final dance at the end of a hangman's rope, my one and only regret was that we never made it to Redemption Valley. I always thought I had more time. It was obvious now I could not have been more wrong.

When the moon was directly overhead, the Marshal took the second watch with a wave of his right hand. Without speaking, he replaced me in the shadows of the aspens.

Walk With Ghost woke up as I lay down beside her and she gave me a tender kiss on my lips and mouthed, "I love you" before drifting back off to sleep. My mind once again was filled only with thoughts of my wife and what would become of her once I was gone.

Thinking about what was best for Walk With Ghost, I decided once we got to Denver I would have the Marshal contact Lucas and Devon Eldridge in Central City and try and contact Chance Bondurant and Kellie Shawn over in Hot Sulphur Springs about seeing to her welfare once the U.S. Cavalry boys were done with me. It was a comfort knowing that those friends that would be contacted were some of the finest and most honorable people I have ever known and that they would do what was right for Walk

With Ghost. If she wanted, I am sure she could live out her life with these friends. If she wanted to return to the tribe and her brother, Chief Piah on the reservation in Utah, I had full confidence that our friends would make that happen.

Having decided on this course of action, I felt like a huge weight had been lifted off my shoulders and I quickly fell to sleep.

CHAPTER 38

Waking before the sunrise, I was on alert. Today we would encounter those that had slaughtered the homesteaders.

The air was slightly chilled with a slight northern wind that brought the smell of the river up into our encampment; it smelled fresh and earthy just as it always does just before rain. The sky had filled during the time I had been sleeping with dark and angry clouds. Looking to the sky and the heavens, I knew it was not about if it would rain; it was about when and how much. The songbirds were silent this morning and content to save their singsong melodies for a better day.

Moving out of the bedroll and away from the now awakening Walk With Ghost, I stood and stretched my arms and legs with actually little or no pain. It was the first time since my deadly encounter with Doug Webb the bounty hunter that had me feeling close to normal. I felt so much better; in fact, it made me chuckle some and I took a slight bow toward Marshal Robert's sugar sack containing the head of the late legendary bounty hunter. I said to no one in particular, but meant for the deceased, "Feeling just a tad chipper this morning Dougie Boy! Hope you were able to rest your sleepy head."

The Marshal was strapping on his holster and sidearm and apparently did not see the humor of my good tidings toward the recently departed and did an eye roll. I took that as my signal to start strapping on my own Colt.

After getting my weapons ready for the day ahead, we took the time, after bringing the horses in so that we could saddle them, to rub them down with a curry comb. I think it went a long ways toward getting Cimarron on the Matt Lee team. I got the feeling that Webb never took the time to care and show love towards the muscular beast. Cimarron nuzzled me with her long face after I was done with the curry comb and if I was a betting man, I would have said that was a first for the legendary horse. Just my luck, I would get to the point of loving this horse and letting her love me back just before my final dance at the end of a rope. Life and its mysterious and most of the time dangerous ride!

Dawn had broken with no sunshine since it was still hiding behind the ever darkening rain clouds. I was even more pleased to be able to step into the stirrup and get my butt planted in the saddle on the first attempt. Walk With Ghost with a smile and a small clap of her hands said, "I am impressed old man."

Stopping as I moved from Cimarron next to Spirit and Walk With Ghost, I leaned over and gave my wife a quick kiss before I took point and started toward the trail heading east.

About a quarter of a mile down the trail, I heard the "caw, caw" before I saw the big black crow. The crow was a monster and probably twice the size of any other crow I had ever seen in the Rockies. He was sitting on a stout evergreen branch, his eyes never blinking as I rode past him. This one for sure was a messenger sent from the "Great Spirit" and was a dire warning of events to come and usually that meant some death would be in the offering. I was feeling so good; I knew it would not be mine.

By mid-morning it started to sprinkle with a slight mist and the air turned colder, but the mist had not dampened the air enough to prevent the smell of wood smoke.

My nose told me there was a campfire ahead of us and Cimarron snorted once as if to warn me. Her eyes were alert and her ears stood straight up, so I reached down to pat her lovingly on her neck to assure her that I had understood her warning and she then dropped her head twice as if saying "okay." I am not sure how Doug Webb had become the owner of this horse, but she was one magnificent animal and it was a privilege to be riding her.

Pulling back slightly on the reins to come to a stop, I held my right hand up in a closed fist to indicate for the Marshal and Walk With Ghost to stop also. We were close to those that had butchered the homestead family we buried yesterday. It would almost be assured that those responsible would not lay down their arms and come peacefully. Marshal Eric Robert was in control and it would be his play when we encounter the outlaws; my presence here was as his back-up.

Marshal Robert and I both switched to our moccasins for noiseless movement through the wood. With the buckskin moccasins you could feel every tree branch and twig before you stepped hard enough to snap and send a message to those we were hunting.

We did not speak for fear the sound would carry for a great distance in the silence of the woods. I indicated with hand signals that Walk With Ghost should stay with the horse and make sure her Winchester was loaded in case she needed it.

The Marshal indicated for me to take the lead not because as a prisoner he wanted to keep an eye on me, but instead because he trusted my woodcraft more than his own. He knew my promise to him about not causing him any grief on the trail was good as gold and that I would honor it to the end. If not for the fact he was taking me in for the murder of those four troopers, we would have become great friends and allies.

The wet mist and the slight drizzle had dampened the floor of the woods and made it a soft and almost noiseless cushion as we approached our new adversaries. Because it was only mid-morning, it told me the cowardly butchers had not moved their camp from last night and probably were content to wait out the day for nicer weather for traveling.

Moving cautiously and inching our way closer to the point, we could actually see the smoke from the outlaw's campfire as it wafted through the trees. It was not long after seeing the smoke that I could hear muted voices and the sounds of their horses as they snorted and stomped their hooves every once in a while.

The outlaw horses had not sensed our presence yet and if they were farm or town horses, they might not ever sense our closeness. That is why I always liked to choose an Indian horse born in the wilderness, because their senses were more in tune with the wilderness and predators. And make no mistake about it the Marshal and I are the predators today.

I had reached a point where I could see into the camp through the aspen and evergreen trees giving me a view as if I was looking between the slats in a wood picket fence. The horses were tied off to a picket line to my far right and two of the men were standing warming themselves by the fire while the third man was tending to the horses' needs. All three men were armed with Colt pistols on their right sides with hand grips pointing backwards for a standard draw. The third man also had his Winchester rifle leaning on an aspen tree close by.

After studying the men for several minutes, I thought them to be all kin, for they all had the same likeness and manner about them. The two outlaws warming themselves by the fire might even be twins. Their hair was long past their shoulders and dark brown, dirty, and with leaves and twigs imbedded as if they had been there awhile. They both wore blue jeans and long sleeve buckskin shirts that seemed to have never been clean from the day they had been made. Their weapons, the Colts they wore, and the only Winchester that was visible to my eye, did however look to be well taken care of and absent of dirt and or rust. The third outlaw that was tending to the horses was dressed the exact same as the other two. The only difference was he was older and maybe their Pa or an Uncle. I had no doubt that they were all related in some way and would have the same way of thinking, which made them even more dangerous.

After seeing the lay of the land and the outlaw camp, I felt it would be a sound move for me to enter the campsite from the far left and complete opposite side of the horses, putting me roughly 60 feet apart from Marshal Eric Robert as he would enter from the trail. With hand signals I relayed my thoughts to the Marshal and he shook his head with approval. I then signaled him to give me ten minutes until I was in position.

Still with stealth and woodcraft, I moved to the far left cautiously, not wanting to give away our presence as I moved slightly further back in the timber so no movement could be seen through the trees. In doing this I would not be able to see into the camp until I was in position.

Once I felt I had put 60 or more feet in between the Marshal and myself, I turned toward the camp and moved straight for it until I could once again see into the outlaw's camp. The problem was the third man and his Winchester was no longer in my eyesight, and I was not sure from the Marshal's vantage point if he could see him or had ever seen him. This could be a costly mistake.

As much as I studied the trees surrounding the campsite, I could not locate the outlaw with the Winchester. I do not believe they had felt or noticed our closeness because the other two men were still in the same position warming themselves by the fire. But the fact of the matter was the third and older desperado was not to be seen.

Just as I was hoping the Marshal would wait until the other man could be seen, he walked right into their campsite and their eyesight with his Colt drawn, saying in a deep and serious voice, "If you boys want to live you will drop those gun belts. You are under arrest."

CHAPTER 39

S oon as the Marshal had made his move into the outlaw camp, I moved swiftly and palmed my Colt covering the two outlaws by the campfire. My eyes were searching every shadow and possible hiding point for the older outlaw with the Winchester.

Both men by the fire turned to face the Marshal since he had been the one to speak. After viewing this movement and seeing their profile, I was more convinced now than ever they were indeed twins, identical twins in fact.

Before another word could be said in the tense moment, I saw movement to the far right of the Marshal as the older outlaw raised his Winchester to fire.

The older outlaw fired his rifle at the Marshal before I could turn to face this threat. Eric Robert was so focused on the twins at the campfire he never saw the third and older brigand.

The older outlaw's bullet caught the Marshal in his right side down low and he stumbled once before he went down to one knee.

Once the first shot was fired, all hell broke loose as the desperado twins went for their Colts. Firing from my hip, I caught the twin on the far left just above his belt buckle before he cleared leather with his sidearm. Raising my Colt, I fanned it not once but twice more as both bullets found a home just below the left twin's throat and as his body started to crumble, my third hit him in his upper lip below the nose killing him instantly.

The second twin had cleared leather and fired at the Marshal as he was on one knee then started to turn on me. The second twin caught my first round in his chest which caused him to drop his weapon to the wet mushy ground as he stumbled backwards. His look was one of bewilderment as he now was within shaking hands of death. At the count of two he face planted into the campfire. The fire ignited his long scraggly and dirty hair as the outlaw died a fitting death. Knowing both twins were down and out of the fight, I tried to concentrate on locating the older outlaw who had fired his rifle and faded out of sight back into the tree line.

In just a few seconds I took all in account of the situation that was now presented before me. The misty rain was still misting and the air had a smell of wetness and burning hair. The Marshal had been wounded and down, but moving and very much alive. The two outlaw twins were both out of the ruckus and dead. I had fired four rounds and had two left in my Colt. I stepped back into the tree line and out of the line of fire and reloaded my pistol before holstering it.

Considering the fact that just several weeks ago I myself was near death, I was feeling pretty good and near being my old self. Taking my Bowie knife silently out of his sheath on my right side, I began the hunt...the way the legend "Ghost" would have hunted.

As I moved closer to the Marshal, the only sound the woods were making was that of the Marshal himself as he struggled to move himself by sliding on the wet and muddy ground behind the cover of an evergreen tree.

Moving within earshot of the Marshal, but keeping focused on the woods surrounding me, I spoke in a whisper to the wounded Eric Robert, "How bad is it?"

The Marshal gritted his teeth as he replied, "I will live, a through and through in the back part of my right thigh and a burning graze on the side of my face that will leave a hell of a scar."

My attention was on the woods for movement or sound as I spoke once again to the wounded Marshal, "You were not what I would have called handsome anyway Marshal."

With pain in the Marshal's voice, "Matt Lee!"

Feeling better knowing the Marshal's wounds were not life threatening, "Yes, Eric Robert?"

Sucking a little air before he spoke again, "Kill that son of a bitch."

Sensing movement without actually seeing it, I moved silently with stealth and woodcraft to the right while saying, "That's my intention Eric Robert."

The hunt for the outlaw and the years of living the life as "Ghost" flooded all my senses and emotions. In this moment of time I felt renewed as my sense of touch, hearing, and eyesight seemed to sharpen - I felt almost as if I had stepped back 30 years in time.

This outlaw, the older one of those that had butchered and slaughtered the homesteaders so savagely and had tried to take the life of Marshal Eric Robert, was now in a death match that I knew he was not suited for. He was facing a different Matt Lee, the one the Utes called "Ghost," the one who survived numerous hand-to-hand combats against those that wanted to take his life. On this day and at this moment I was no longer the old man called Matt Lee that had lost the fight to the bounty hunter Webb. I was now "Ghost" - master of the woods.

Working my way toward what my gut instinct was telling me was the correct direction, I tried to hear or see anything that would give away the older desperado's hiding place. Slowly and with silence, stepping on the cold, wet forest floor feeling every little twig and stone beneath my feet, I made my advance.

Having moved more than 20 yards now away from where the Marshal was sitting with his back to the evergreen tree, I finally caught some movement out of the corner of my eye as the rain went from a cold misting now to an actual icy rain. The movement that had crossed my eye was the outlaw's exhale as his breath clouded in the cold, wet spring air. Now the sound of the outlaw's heavy breathing made its way to my ears. He was taking in short breaths as he tried to calm his fears of knowing he was being hunted in combination of not knowing where the hunter was.

Now knowing where the outlaw was, I used all my skill and all my knowledge of the woods to move within 20 feet of the butcher of the weak. Close enough, I could smell the older renegade's fear as he cradled his Winchester as if it would save him.

The older outlaw was standing with his back to a large evergreen tree and was holding his Winchester tight to his chest with the barrel slightly tipped to the left and away from his face. His face was also turned to the left as he looked and listened to the woods for the one that hunted him. I was 20 feet in front of him and he could not see me; his woodcraft, if he had any, had failed him.

Stepping forward unhurriedly out of the shadows, I stood so he could see me. If I had owned a watch, it would have ticked 20 times before the outlaw turned toward me; he was startled, almost dropping his Winchester as I appeared out of the mist and the rain.

As soon as his mind caught up with his eyesight that there was a man in front of him, it was already too late for the butcher of the homesteaders and helpless. I moved with ghost-like speed and delivered a killing blow with my Bowie knife as it entered his chest in an upward thrust just below the peak of his rib cage in the vicinity of his heart. Now chest to chest with the dying outlaw, I watched his life melt away from his eyes as I turned my Bowie knife once it nicked his heart. Without a word ever spoken between myself and the now dead outlaw, he slowly crumbled to the wet forest floor.

Feeling no joy or pleasure in the death of the three butchers other than the fact that it had been a job that needed to be done, it was a fitting death and probably more honorable than all three of the outlaws deserved. Pulling my knife loose from the outlaw's chest, I cleaned the blood from the blade on the dead outlaw's buckskin shirt before returning it to its sheath.

Moving quickly back to the tree that the wounded Marshal was sitting with his back against, I whistled the sound of a mountain chickadee so Walk With Ghost would know that it was safe to bring Cimarron, Spirit, and Creek. I needed some supplies from our packs to tend to Marshal Eric Robert's wounds.

CHAPTER 40

Two days after tending to the Marshal's wounds with tree moss and pine needles salve, he was well enough to ride, although with some discomfort in his right thigh.

In two days we would make Denver if the weather held so I could begin my time behind bars waiting for the subsequent trial. This of course was not a pleasant thought, but it was what I had agreed to after Marshal Eric Robert had saved Walk With Ghost's and my life. I would ride the final miles with honor and my head held high for in my heart, I knew I had done nothing wrong when I bested those soldier boys in Grand Lake. Civilization had rendered justice in the Rocky Mountain frontier, something that I could not recognize anymore and would be dealt out by judges and lawyers that had never spent one night under the stars in the sky or huddled up to a campfire freezing on a cold high country winter night. In the long haul, maybe the courts and the ensuing hangman were doing me a favor by putting this aging mountain man to rest.

Even with all the madness, blood, and death that had filled a large portion of my life, my one and only regret was I would never make Redemption Valley the last home for Walk With Ghost and myself. She deserved better than me and a better life than I had provided.

The morning of our departure westward to Denver was a crisp and clear morning with not one cloud dotting the sky. As the glorious warming sun rose in the west, it reminded me that each morning of every day was a new beginning, but that in a short 24 hours there would also be an end. In my adventures I was thankful for each and every day I spent above ground, especially knowing how many wanted to take my head over the years.

I had snared a couple of rabbits that night before and Walk With Ghost roasted us up a fine breakfast of some fried beans and some campfire tortillas. Marshal Eric Robert had not spoken much since our deadly encounter with the outlaws that had slaughtered the homestead family. He was dealing with his wounds of course, but he was also in deep thought as the days had progressed. It was not until we had saddled the horses and fed them some grain that he finally broke his self-imposed silence.

Standing next to his mare Creek and with his hand on the saddle to take some of the weight off of his wounded leg, he turned to Walk With Ghost and myself and started speaking in a slow and thoughtful manner, "I have been brooding over what happened in Grand Lake with those dead troopers and in my heart I know that you Matt Lee did nothing that I would not have done myself. I believe in that moment when you fired and killed the first trooper, it was not done with malice and hatred, but done defending your wife's life and both of your honor. Taking a man's life or those lives of those troopers and everything that they would ever be is a tough decision and as I have pondered over and over what happened, I myself can find no fault in what you did."

The Marshal was still in deep thought as he was looking at us. He almost seemed relieved to be getting off his chest what had been bothering him the whole time since the day of the bounty hunter Doug Webb's death. "Having said that, I believe it is my duty as an officer of the territorial court to bring you in for justice and let the court hopefully make the right judgement of what happened that day on the streets of Grand Lake. I reckon this time,

I have a problem with that because I will not be handing you over to the territorial court, but the military court which will have jurisdiction in this case. I fear it will not go well for you there. The U.S. Cavalry's interest is not and will not be justice for your wife Matt Lee. Their concern will be how to resolve this mess with the death of those young lads as quickly and quietly as possible. They will not want a long trial talking about what really happened and bring in the obvious U.S. Cavalry and the white man's hate for the Indians. They will not want it to be known that one man bested so many of their troopers. They will hang you or put you in front of a firing squad as quickly as they can. They will wash away the shame of what the U.S. Cavalry troopers did that day with your death. Sometimes the hardest decision and the right decision are one and the same. I believe this is one of those times. You are free to go. Go home to your Redemption Valley."

Marshal Eric Robert's words had meaning and thought behind them and they also were heartfelt. It truly had been a moral dilemma for him to make that decision.

Walk With Ghost exhaled a gasp and she quickly grabbed my arm almost as if she was going to faint. Looking at my wife and seeing the hope and happiness that was so evident in her face brought me a hesitant smile.

After I watched the Marshal struggle with his inner thoughts the last several weeks, his announcement really was no surprise to me. The last thing I wanted to do was dash that hope for a better future that Walk With Ghost was experiencing right now, but I had also done some heavy pondering since my near death at the hands of Webb the bounty hunter.

If Walk With Ghost and I rode out of here and headed for Redemption Valley, we would forever be looking over our shoulders; the warrant and bounty money would always be there for those willing to try and track me down. And for $2000 cash money, there would always be someone wanting that type of payday and more likely than not the reputation for killing the legend "Ghost." I was not so sure the best course of action after much thought was to repeat what I had done over 30 years ago with Walk With Ghost's brother Chief Piah when I offered my life to him and go ahead and have the trial - and live or die with the outcome. Either clear my name or die at the end of a hangman's rope. It was my thought for all of those that know me that my honor would be intact for having done the honorable thing even in the end if it was death that waited for me. Having those that still wanted my head and the bounty still riding the Colorado Territory looking for me after my near death in the fight with Doug Webb was now not an option. Somehow, someway, I needed to be free of the territorial court's warrant for my arrest.

If not for how much this affected Walk With Ghost's life, I would ride down into Denver with honor and let the military court decide my fate. Looking into the eyes of the one that held my heart and I loved like no other, I was torn on what to do at this point.

Before I could roll it around some more in my mind, fate and destiny played its hand. Cimarron snorted twice and pawed the ground with her front right hoof as she was forewarned before I was. Looking in the direction she was now looking, I caught movement not far to the east of us and heading our way.

Walk With Ghost went to pull her Winchester from her saddle scabbard. Keeping my eyes to the east and tracking ten horses that were heading towards us, I reached out and stopped her. I was willing to let chance and destiny play this out without bloodshed this time.

It would appear that the U.S. Cavalry had not given up its search for the killer of their troopers. I had a gut feeling these hard men riding U.S. Cavalry mounts were looking for me - Matt Lee. The troopers that now rode in and stood before us still mounted in their saddles in a half circle were not the same green as grass troopers that had been tracking the Utes and of those in Grand Lake.

These ten troopers down to the last man were battle hardened veterans of war and fully armed with repeating rifles and Colt firearms. You could read in their faces that all were as tough as they come and older and had probably served fighting for one side or the other in the Civil War. Each and every one of them was a warrior bar none. And the man that was leading them was none other than Master Sergeant Andy Cacy, the very same Master Sergeant that knew me and what I looked like.

CHAPTER 41

Marshal Robert, still standing by his mare Creek, gave me a concerned sideways glance as he pulled back his vest revealing his gold star with the word Marshal stamped on it so the newcomers could see it. It was evident to me that the Master Sergeant was in charge by how the other soldiers deferred to let him and his mount step forward slightly ahead of the others.

The Master Sergeant was a man accustomed to leading other men and it was obvious he was no fool. In the first seconds of gaining our camp, I could see his eyes flash in between the Marshal's star and the fact that I was armed with my Colt tucked away in its holster on my side and carrying my Winchester rifle. His face showed one of total bewilderment as he cautiously placed his right hand on his holstered sidearm. I studied him as he studied me and I could see and feel his confusion of the moment as he was trying to put all he saw in some sort of order in his mind. If not for the possibility of my death from one Master Sergeant Andy Cacy and these battle hardened soldiers, this whole encounter would be downright humorous.

Walk With Ghost gathered up close to me without speaking and touched my hand gingerly as it hung by my side. I could feel her palm sweat from the tension that was now in the air. I was surprised at how calm I actually was. It seemed as if the good Lord or the Great Spirit had brought my life full circle to this very moment in time. My life and or death would be decided on this spot east of Kenosha pass next to the South Platte River. And I was perfectly fine with that.

With so much riding on what happened in the next several minutes, I took in all that surrounded me in the way of nature. The sky was filled with fine-looking fluffy white clouds as the morning sun was still in the eastern horizon warming the spring air and the earth. The recent rain had given all things in the wilderness an extra boost of scent and the pine of the evergreens as well as the aspen trees flooded my senses so much that I could actually taste them. The South Platte River was running full to the top of its banks from the recent rain and the snowmelt that trickled down from above timberline and the sound of water rushing over the boulders and rocks was a refreshing sound to me as if all was being washed and cleaned for a new beginning. The wind picked up as if on cue to make the aspens quake with the "tree whispers" that I loved so well. It was a wonderful day to be alive and a good day to die if it came down to that. I attentively held Walk With Ghost's hand in mine as if to tell her no matter what happens now that I was okay with it and so should she.

The Marshal spoke first and in a clear and loud voice, "My name is Eric Robert and I am one of the territorial marshals of Colorado. What can I do for you today Master Sergean?"

By his introduction I was surprised that the Marshal and the Master Sergeant did not know each other. They either had been in Grand Lake during or in the case of Master Sergeant Cacy shortly after my shootout with those four U.S. Cavalry troopers. With all the commotion of what was going on at the time, it was possible that both men had never crossed paths.

Master Sergeant Cacy was slow to respond as he looked at me and it showed on his face that he knew exactly who I was as he spoke, "Marshal, my name is Master Sergeant Andy Cacy and after being refitted and given more experienced men at Fort Sheridan, these men and I have been given the mission of tracking down and arresting the man Matt Lee, the one the Ute Indians call Ghost. He is wanted in connection with the death of four troopers in Grand Lake, Colorado."

The tension had risen for those in the know. I for one was not going to fight these men and I knew that, but Andy Cacy could not have known that. The nine troopers with Cacy were oblivious to what was really happening at this very moment. Master Sergeant Cacy, Walk With Ghost, and I were on edge and we all were seeing how this played out. I could also see, feel, and hear the tension in Marshal Eric Robert as he was about to do something that would be difficult for him being the man that he was. Looking directly at the Master Sergeant, Marshal Robert spoke again, "Looking for the famous Matt Lee? Look no further Master Sergeant, he is here and I have him."

Walk With Ghost's hand tightened as she held mine, and her fingernails now dug into the palm of my hand. Master Sergeant Cacy seemed not at all fazed by the Marshal's statement and the other nine battle hardened troopers now looked confused as their hands instinctively went to their side arms.

Cacy kept his eye on me waiting for any movement from me. If he was expecting any, he would be disappointed because I was fully ready to be arrested here and now if that is what fate and destiny had for me. I kept my arms to my side holding my wife's hand.

The only one that moved at all, and it was not a sudden movement, was Marshal Robert as he dug into his pack behind his saddle on his mare Creek and produced the sugar sack that contained the now mummified head of the bounty hunter Doug Webb. Now it was my turn to be confused as the Marshal turned and tossed the sugar sack to the Master Sergeant. "Matt Lee is dead, and here is his head as proof. I was going to showcase it in Denver as soon as I got there."

Master Sergeant Cacy was so astonished that he almost failed to catch the sugar sack containing Webb's head and fumbled it twice before gaining a good hold of it.

Marshal Robert turned to me and rolled his eyes, raising his eyebrow in such a manner as if to say, "Hell, if I am going to lie, it might as well be a big one."

The absurdity of the Marshal telling a lie and the fact Master Sergeant Cacy already knew it to be bullshit brought a smile to my face and I had to stop myself from actually laughing out loud. Of course Walk With Ghost's body was a hard knot of tension as the possibility that the end of my life would play out here on the bank of the South Platte River.

From the look on the Master Sergeant's confused face, he was having a difficult time deciding whether to shoot me or ride over and shake my hand. What he did was open the sugar sack containing Webb's head.

He finally moved his eyes from me to the sugar sack as he looked at the mummified head of the late Doug Webb. Several seconds passed before he turned his eyes from what the sugar sack contained, and he looked at Marshal Eric Robert, turning his attention once again towards me before he spoke, "Not sure if you know this Marshal Robert, but I actually have met the legend Matt Lee."

This tad bit of information did not bode well with the Marshal and he slowly put his hand on the butt of his Colt pistol. The Marshal did however just for a second glance my way and if his glance could have spoken, it would have said, "Thanks for mentioning that - you asshole."

CHAPTER 42

Master Sergeant Cacy locked eyes with me for what seemed several minutes, but I am sure it was only a few seconds. He rested the sugar sack containing the remains of the bounty hunter in front of his saddle horn on his U.S. Cavalry mount's mane. "You know Marshal Robert, it is difficult to tell if this poor bastard in the sugar sack was the man the Ute Indians called "Ghost." Half his face is full of buckshot and the whole head has dried up looking like a prune. Lacking the body of the fugitive, I would not be able to say for sure it was Matt Lee. I am curious as how you happened to have these remains?"

The other nine battle-hardened troopers to a man looked confused and flummoxed at what was playing out in front of them. I took comfort in the fact no one had pulled a sidearm and started throwing 44 slugs all over the place - at least not yet. Since the Master Sergeant had not given up the Marshal's ruse of yet, the

Marshal looked my way once again and upped the ante on his bold outright lie. With a wink only meant for Walk With Ghost and myself and his hand still resting on the butt of his Colt, he spoke once again, "Won't bore you with details Master Sergeant Cacy and will keep it short; I trailed Matt Lee from Grand Lake after receiving a territorial warrant for his arrest in the connection of the death of those troopers you spoke of. What I did not know was the famous bounty hunter named Doug Webb had started trailing him a day or two before I did. I caught up with both them at the top of Kenosha Pass. From the signs of the battle that had taken place, both men had given it their all before they both succumbed to the wounds that had been afflicted from the other one. I would have paid top dollar to see these two famous men fight it out, but sadly I got there after the fighting and killing was done. After relieving Matt Lee of his head, I buried both bodies on top of Kenosha in unmarked graves."

Feeling Walk With Ghost sway a little from a momentary faint, I grabbed her arm to keep her upright. She regained her footing and I felt her muscles kick in as she was able to maintain standing without propping her up. I then let her go to free up my gun hand. I did not want this to turn into a shooting match and I would go peacefully, but I would and could not let Walk With Ghost or the Marshal get shot. If I had to protect them, I would.

Being impressed with the story that the Marshal had just spun brought a slight smile to my face. A lie with just enough truth that if the Master Sergeant had not known me, he might have bought it. Hell, I almost bought the story myself.

Master Sergeant Cacy looked at me once again, and his eyes drifted down to my mount Cimarron. Of course he recognized the most famous horse in the Rocky Mountain frontier and by the story the Marshal had spun, he now knew that the head in the sugar sack was that of Doug Webb the bounty hunter. Instead of reaching for his sidearm, he once again opened the sugar sack and looked in for what seemed like a long spell. Nodding his head twice in a "yes" motion, he closed up the sack and tied it behind his saddle horn. Then he leaned forward in a non-threatening manner, looking directly at Walk With Ghost and myself and spoke in a clear and confident voice, "Marshal Robert, Matt Lee alias "Ghost" had a distinctive head of white hair and after looking a second time, I reckon I can positively identify this head in the sack as the wanted fugitive Matt Lee."

With an audible sigh of relief, Marshal Eric Robert replied, "I am glad Master Sergeant Cacy this matter with Matt Lee is now a closed incident and the both of us can get on doing what we do best in trying to keep the Colorado Territory and the frontier safe."

Trying not to give Master Sergeant Cacy a chance to second guess himself, Walk With Ghost, Marshal Eric Robert, and I mounted our horses since they were already saddled when the troopers rode in.

Once saddled Master Sergeant Cacy gave his mount a slight jab with his spur and rode up in between Walk With Ghost and myself. Once close enough, he reached out his hand and I grasped it with all my strength. Out of the corner of my eye, I could see the tears start to flow down Walk With Ghost's face. Looking me straight in the eye as men that respect each other do, Master Sergeant Cacy spoke, "You sir, have an uncanny resemblance to someone I use to know and had the highest respect for. I just found out a short time ago that this man has recently passed on and I just wanted to shake your hand. I did not catch your name."

Holding his hand tight in friendship and understanding, I replied, "I reckon I didn't give it son."

Master Sergeant Cacy's face broke into a smile as he continued, "This man who passed, I met him in the Kawuneeche Valley and have thought of him from time to time and if he were still alive, I would have told him he had been a hero and a legend to many, including myself here in the Rocky Mountains. That I understood the troubles that had plagued him down through the years and here just recently were never of his own making. His heart, I know, was pure and he was as tough as they come and I for one will miss him very much."

After releasing my grip, Walk With Ghost still with tears in her eyes and staining her face bent over and kissed the Master Sergeant on his cheek.

As Marshal Eric Robert, Master Sergeant Cacy, and the remaining troopers reined their horses toward the east and Denver, Walk With Ghost and I reined Spirit and Cimarron westward toward Redemption Valley. We overheard one of the U.S. Cavalry troopers say to Master Sergeant Cacy, "What the hell was that all about?"

Looking back over my shoulder, I could see the Master Sergeant looking back over his toward me as he spoke to his trooper, "Shut up Joe!"

EPILOGUE

S ince I left Marshal Eric Robert, Master Sergeant Andy Cacy, and the rest of the U.S. Cavalry troopers on the banks of the South Platte River, the spring and summer months had faded into the autumn months. After the slow decay of summer, the autumn to me was the most pleasing and beautiful time of year. The Lord had seen fit to put on an awe-inspiring display of colors both in the leaves and the skies that every day, while finishing our cabin in Redemption Valley, Walk With Ghost and I would stop working for a spell and bask in the beauty of the falling leaves and the color all around us. The days of the "tree whispers" would soon be over once the last leaf had fallen from its branch, and I would miss their mountain melodies until next year. The air was turning cool and crisp this morning under a cloudless, sunny sky and we could see our breath.

We had been busy and the wood pile was deep enough for us to survive the upcoming winter months, and we had enough food stored to get us through the tough days ahead. The only task left was finishing a corral for Spirit and Cimarron, which we had been working on for the last couple of days.

As I was working the handmade posthole digger, Walk With Ghost touched my arm and pointed toward the north and the hidden entrance into Redemption Valley.

Seeing the movement of something dark moving through the trees, I quickly grabbed my holster and Colt which I had hung on the last fence post I had planted and strapped them on. Walk With Ghost picked up the Winchester and used the lever action to load a shell into the firing chamber. We had gotten comfortable knowing nobody was looking for me since the legend "Ghost" had died on Kenosha Pass and the territorial warrant would no longer be valid. Seeing this movement, I hoped and prayed the past had not beaten a path to our home here in Redemption Valley.

The movement turned out to be a lone wolf, and he was not using any stealth as he made his way quickly through the trees until he finally stopped at my feet. Correction, not wolf, but a half wolf and half something else dog. Chance's dog Mutt was sitting in front of me wagging his tail and hoping to be petted, which Walk With Ghost did with the biggest smile on her face I had seen in a long time.

I waited until all four horses carrying Chance, Kellie Shawn, Devon, and Lucas - my only true friends in the world - came to a halt. Friends that I thought I would never see again, friends who would have thought that I was long dead. Each and every one of them had a shit eating grin that probably matched my own plastered on their faces when Lucas broke the silence and said, "Well, hell, look at that Chance, if it isn't a real "Ghost." Chance and I never believed that story you had been killed, and we put bits and pieces of the stories you told of us about this valley and we got a wild hair to come looking. I knew you were too cantankerous and ornery to die Matt Lee without saying goodbye to your friends. Having seen you though, I would have to say you look like shit."

Laughing out loud for the first time in - hell - I couldn't remember the last time I laughed out loud, "Well Lucas, you should have seen the other guy! Now that you have found us, what do you plan on doing?"

After Chance, Kellie Shawn, Devon, and Lucas dismounted, Lucas said, "I bet you have been making Walk With Ghost do all the work so it looks like we got a corral to finish building to give her some much needed rest."

Walking up to my friend who had tears of joy in his eyes that somehow seemed trivial to my own tears, I grabbed him and hugged him tight, "I reckon so Lucas, I reckon so."

Author Note: La Caverna Del Oro
The story that inspired "Rocky Mountain Ghost"

I always wanted to write a fictional novel about the La Caverna Del Oro. Please note the legend to follow is somewhat documented and some is conjecture on my part. I do not claim it to be the absolute truth. I originally published this article on Hubpages on July 19th, 2015.

La Caverna Del Oro (The Cave of Gold)

As a young boy growing up in Denver, Colorado in the 1960's and 1970's, I never could even imagine the prospects of owning a computer, smart phone or an Ipad. I did not even see color TV until my grandparents got a color set when I was about 10 or 11 years old. I played outside, read books by flipping pages, and I would always listen to stories that were told and passed on by the older generation. By far my favorite stories of my youth were those told to me of lost treasure and ghosts.

The first time I ever heard the story La Caverna Del Oro (The Cave of Gold) it was told to me by a stranger, an older gentleman while we were both waiting to get our hair cut at Stoney's Barber Shop at Federal and Hampden in Sheridan, Colorado south of downtown Denver. I was clutching my $1.25 which also included the tip that my Mom had sent with me to pay the barber "Old Man Stoney." As we waited the older man waiting for his haircut began the tale.

In the beginning

Caverna Del Oro was 13,000 feet high upon the present day Marble Mountain and long before the United States was the United

States, a tale, a legend was passed down by generation after generation of the local Indians of a cave that was protected by demons high up on the mountain just above timberline. What the demons protected they did not know, but all that would venture into the cave never returned. The Indians thought the cave was evil and ate their loved ones.

In 1541, three monks from the Spanish Coronado expedition while exploring in what is now present day Colorado (Spanish for the color red), heard from the Indians a tale they recorded about the mysterious cave high up on the mountain. Intrigued the monks, doing what monks did during the 15th century, enslaved the Indians and forced them to locate the demon cave. Upon discovery of the cave, the monks also found what they were truly looking for and that was gold - gold and riches beyond belief. Forced into labor, the Indians mined the gold from the demon cave. Since the cave was located high above timberline, it could only be mined in the summer months due to heavy snow during the winter. So the Spanish whipped and beat their slave Indians to try and get them to work faster.

Revolt and massacre

After being enslaved and beaten by the Spanish monks for that long summer, the Indians revolted and attacked the heavily armed Spanish, and all the Indians were killed except one who escaped to tell the story of what had happened at the demon cave.

But during the Indian slave revolt, the Indians inflicted some damage on the Spanish and killed two of the monks. The remaining monk whose name was De La Cruz and the surviving members of the expedition packed the gold on their pack animals which was in those days a vast amount of gold and returned southward to Mexico before the cold and snow of the harsh mountain winter came blowing down from the north.

The Spanish never returned to La Caverna Del Oro. It was said that De La Cruz, the only surviving monk of the ill-fated expedition and the only one who knew the exact location of the gold mine in the Sangre de Cristo Mountains of what is now southwestern Colorado, caught a fever upon his return to Mexico and died.

Maybe he brought the demon back with him or maybe it was justice in the end that prevailed.

The Indians also never returned to La Caverna Del Oro as they thought of it as the demon cave where so much pain and suffering had been inflicted upon their loved ones.

Over the years the location was forgotten, but never the tale.

Nuggets and gold bars discovered

In 1811, 270 years later a man named Baca, while exploring in the Sangre de Cristo Mountains in the vicinity of Marble Mountain, stumbled upon a stash of mined gold nuggets and some rugged and primitive made gold bars, which in my mind raises the question, "Did in fact De La Cruz the Spanish monk and the surviving members of the expedition make it back to Mexico? If the first part of the story is true, where did the already mined nuggets and primitive gold bars come from?"

Baca had heard the story La Caverna Del Oro from some local Indians and continued to search for the location of the haunted gold mine, but he never did find the location or entrance to the mine. Baca recorded his find in his expedition journal.

La Caverna Del Oro rediscovered?

In 1869, a man named Elisha P. Horn while he was exploring Marble Mountain discovered a cave. And according to a reporter and Elisha's own journal of the event, he supposedly found a skeleton near the cave's entrance clad in Spanish armor. Elisha also observed an arrow that had pierced the armor, apparently killing its occupant.

Had he stumbled upon the lost La Caverna Del Oro, the cave of gold that the monks and Indians had died for and its golden riches buried deep down in its throat? It was never recorded if Elisha tried to explore the interior of the mine or even if he had even heard the tale of the La Caverna Del Oro.

The cave, gold, secrets, and demon guardian were once again lost to the passage of time.

216

Spanish encampment and the cave of gold found once again?

In the year of our Lord 1880 a man named J.H. Yeoman discovered an ancient fortress at the mouth of a small cave on Marble Mountain. The walls of the fort were constructed of rock and timbers, and rifle pits had been constructed for its defense, which will lead one to suspect that the original story of the Spanish legend and the three monks was in fact a true telling of an ancient but not forgotten story.

Upon further exploration J.H. Yeoman found a much larger cave several hundred yards higher than the abandoned fortress. Was this the demon and haunted cave La Caverna Del Oro? Was he only several hundred feet away from the gold, demons, and a legend?

That night after finding the fortress and the much larger cave, it started to snow and forced J.H. Yeoman down the mountain and to safety. There is no record of J.H. Yeoman ever exploring the interior of the cave.

Another attempt in 1920

In 1920, Paul Gilbert a forest ranger learned of the legend of La Caverna Del Oro from Apollonia Apodaca, who was a direct descendant of the first Spanish explorers that had explored the area around present day Marble Mountain. Apollonia told Paul of the Indian revolt. She went on to explain that as a young girl she and others of her family even visited the cave and were afraid to enter because of a constant wind that blew upward and outward from the mouth and the entrance of the cave. Believing that the wind was the demon who guarded the cave, they never returned. She did tell Paul that at the entrance of the cave there was a red Maltese cross painted on a rock near the entrance.

Paul Gilbert enlisted some of his fellow forest rangers to try and locate the cave, and the following weekend they believed that they did. They did indeed find a very dull red Maltese cross painted on a rock near an entrance of a cave. They also confirmed the mighty wind that blew from the opening. Determined to explore further, they entered the mouth of the cave and explored the first level where they found a pit that headed vertically down a shaft. Not having the proper equipment, they could not explore any further and vowed to explore another day.

Shortly after Paul Gilbert's first and only attempt, he died suddenly of unknown causes.

Legend to reality!

In 1929 the legend of La Caverna Del Oro was told to one Frederick G. Bonfils, who happened to be the co-founder and publisher of the Denver Post. Bonfils became fascinated with the story and decided to finance an expedition of two men to locate and explore the cave.

To explore a cave above timberline at 13,000 feet, you have to remember that the cold and snow are present even in the summer months, and the weather is never your friend. The weather pattern at that altitude can change in a moment's notice making such an expedition a very dangerous endeavor.

Bangles' two man expedition did find the cave with the now very faint Maltese cross and started to explore. They reported that the cave did in fact have a ceaseless wind that howled from the mouth of the mountain, and the howling wind was cold, very intensely cold. The first level was reported to be very steep and muddy with icy spots and very difficult to walk on. The wind with its cold froze the two men's wet gloves on their hands. The omnipresent wind was so loud they found it difficult to speak and to be heard in the cave. As they explored, they found numerous passageways, too many to give an exact count. At the bottom of one deep pit, they found a log that was wedged in between two walls and a ladder made of chain fastened to the log which gave credence to the fact that the Spanish had indeed been in this cave, for the Indians at that time had no knowledge of how to make iron or metal. The chain was very ancient and rusted through and not useable. The men were surprised at the number of passageways and worried about getting lost and stranded in the deep and dark abyss. This also helped in my belief of why the earlier Indian explorers never returned. They could have simply gotten lost and died of exposure. After discovering the vastness of the cave tunnel system, the men soon realized they were ill equipped for such a dangerous expedition. They also reported not seeing any gold or any type of mining activity. My belief is it would have been difficult to recognize any primitive mining activity when the passage of time had been 388 years.

Tired, hungry, and hands frozen, the two men made a hasty but a safe retreat to the entrance of the cave. Outside and away from the roaring wind that bellowed from the depths of the mountain, the two men could finally speak and hold a conversation. Both spoke of feeling an eerie presence and an overall sense of unease within the confines of the mountain cave.

La Caverna Del Oro legend adds a new wrinkle

In 1932 another expedition that was better equipped was launched in an attempt to understand the mysterious cave's cryptic past. This expedition found a vast cave tunnel system and deep into the heart of Marble Mountain the team of explorers found in the bottom of a deep pit a skeleton with a metal strap around its neck and chained to the wall. This poor fellow had been left to die.

And the legend grows

The following weekend after finding the skeleton chained to the wall in 1932 and a lengthy article in the Rocky Mountain News, a group of seven men that included some of Colorado's best cavers and spelunkers made the trip to Marble Mountain.

During the week between expeditions, someone had tried to dynamite the entrance of La Caverna Del Oro in a feeble attempt to close it down. Who did this is still a mystery today.

The group of seven very experienced cavers found several Indian arrowheads at the ancient fortress which supports the legend that the Indians did in fact attack the Spanish Monks.

In one deep pit, the seven explorers found ancient logs with chains attached to them to use as ladders. No nails were used to build the ladders and seemed ancient in design.

They also located a wooden structure that spanned the top of one of the deep pits that was estimated to be 250 feet deep, and this structure they believed was used to hoist ore up from the bottom of the pit.

This expedition also reported finding two wooden doors at a bottom of one of the pits. What was the purpose for the doors and where did this new passage go? There were just too many passages and pits to explore in the short amount of time that they had to explore, not really solving the mystery of the cave, but adding to the already growing legend of La Caverna Del Oro.

The seven too were stunned by the vastness of the cave system inside of Marble Mountain and also experienced the bone chilling cold of the mighty wind that seemed to come not just from one area but an ever deep pit within the cave. The seven also reported a feeling of unease and the presence of something just beyond the reach of their flashlights and torches.

Final thoughts

Even today the cave resists all that breach the entrance. In all the attempts to explore La Caverna Del Oro from the 15th century into modern history, something has gone wrong from the death of the early explorers to modern cavers becoming sick or simply forgetting their caving techniques. All attempts to solve the mystery surrounding the cave have only added more mystery to the ever growing tale. What we do know is that most of the legend now seems believable, but what about the lost gold? Why didn't any of the expeditions find evidence of mining? Why were some left to die all alone and in the dark? Where does the howling wind come from? Is there a demon that lives in the rock and the walls of the cave?

In recent times the search for the answers to the mystery of La Caverna Del Oro have diminished, and it is my belief that is because in all the modern expeditions, no gold was ever discovered which just adds to the mystery. All the expeditions found new puzzles, but no real answers to what really happened over 400 years ago inside the abyss of Marble Mountain.

As a young boy waiting to get his hair cut, I heard this story and from the very first time, the story has never left me. And the little boy that still resides within my body is grateful for that.

AUTHOR'S NOTE CONT.

If you, the reader, have made it this far, that means you have finished reading my book "Rocky Mountain Ghost," and I would just like to take a line or two to thank you for purchasing my work, and I hope you enjoyed the book.

It is my hope you have found Colorado to be a living and breathing character as much as Matt Lee's alias "Ghost" and Walk With Ghost. I love Colorado and everything it offers.

You may ask, "Is the hidden valley named in the story Redemption Valley real?" One thing I know is that Boreas Pass, where the valley is located, I have in my life traveled numerous times, but to reveal if the valley is real would destroy the whole concept of "hidden." If you, the reader wanted to locate "Redemption Valley," you have enough clues in the story to locate it - if it is. Who knows you might run into the kin of Matt Lee and Walk With Ghost.

With maybe the exception of Redemption Valley, I want to assure you that the Colorado geography, along the path my hero Matt Lee and the beautiful Ute Princess Walk With Ghost traveled through the Colorado Mountains, does in fact exist - every mountain, mountain range, mountain pass, town, mining camp, river, and creek.

I took some liberty in using the modern names in some cases or the more historical names if I thought it fit the story better. I wanted folks who were locals or familiar with this Colorado area to be able to follow along on Matt Lee's adventure more easily in their mind and to be able to travel if they wanted to on horseback, foot, or even by car or 4 wheel drive the same path of Matt Lee and Walk With Ghost as they tried to put their past behind them and find sanctuary in Redemption Valley.

The cover photo, as with my previous novels "Rocky Mountain Reckoning" and "Rocky Mountain Retribution" is one of my own taken in Rocky Mountain National Park.

ABOUT THE AUTHOR

Kurt James was born and raised in the foothills of the Colorado Rocky Mountains. With family roots in western Kansas and having lived in South Dakota for 20 years, Kurt James naturally has become an old western and nature enthusiast. Over the years Kurt James has become one of Colorado's prominent nature photographers through his brand name of Midnight Wind Photography. His poetry has been featured in the Denver Post, PM Magazine and on 9NEWS in Denver, Colorado. Kurt James' poetry is also featured at Creative Exiles, a collection of some of the finest poets on the web. Kurt James Reifschneider is also a feature writer for Hubpages with the articles focused on Colorado history, ghost towns, outlaws, and poetry. Inspired at a young age by writers such as Jack London, Louis L'amour and Max Brand, Kurt has formed his natural ability as a story teller. "Rocky Mountain Ghost" is Kurt James' third novel in his Rocky Mountain Series, but not the last novel of the western frontier of the wild and dangerous Colorado Rocky Mountains.

https://www.facebook.com/authorkurtjames/